Scenic Utah

Mike Bahl

Scenic Utah
By Mike Bahl

Edited by Valerie Valentine
Front Cover Photo by Lindsay Gilster
Back Cover Photo by Mike Bahl

"Carbohydrate Coma" first published in *Phraseology*
"Refining My Sense Of Humor" first published in *Opium Magazine*
"Welcome To The Neighborhood" first published in *Barrier Islands Review*

REMEDY INKORPORATED

ISBN 978-1-304-97514-0

For VV, WC, and KC, who have been far and away my biggest supporters. These words wouldn't be here without you. This is the best way I know how to say thank you. You mean a lot to me. Please keep being awesome.

Contents

All Out

"Happy Kimdependence Day!"

A hipster masquerading safely as a hooker for the night stood in front of a plate glass window taller than me. Originally, the window was most likely meant to be a store display. An electronics repair store on one side. A Thai place with apartments above it on the other. Another masquerade; a former retail outlet now an art gallery/living space, now a club for the night. Through the window's cage of thief-proof bars I could see a room bathed in low light and bodies in motion on the dance floor. Abstract animal prints hung on the walls.

The hip-hooker yelled toward me, "Lil' Kim's getting out of jail today!" She had a forty of malt liquor in a paper bag extended high over her head. The bag was half pulled down, proudly displaying the bottle. It was July third, 2006; thus the pun. Hipsters need only the flimsiest reason to throw a party, so one was thrown in honor of the nipple pasty princess's release from prison for good behavior. Suggested attire: fishnets and pasties or, ideally, nothing.

I was uncomfortable with the whole theme. But I really liked getting drunk.

I walked into a hallway that stretched the length of the building. Rooms sprouted off of this hallway, forming a squared-off honeycomb with the hallway at center. I peeked into each room, searching for the only thing that mattered to me, and was assaulted by sleazy white girls in their most Kimtastic apparel. I had to crawl up a fishnetted leg or two to get to the back-left room where the booze was.

I drank four beers before I came—I had to—and wasted no

time pouring myself a bourbon and diet soda from the impromptu bar, which was a folding table with a few bottles of miscellaneous liquors and half-full bottles of wine on top.

I was overwhelmed with faux or real sexuality. I wasn't sure how much of this promiscuity was meant to be a joke, or if joke was the right word. Sexuality cloaked in hipster irony, the sort of irony that is serious on some level, but the orator is afraid to show her true feelings so she pretends like what she feels is a joke, giving everything an aura of truth and of falsehood. A life lived beneath a veil so thick not even the self knows what she feels. I drank to stabilize the world around me, to help illuminate the truth.

My friend Marcus, who had given me a ride to the party, found me camped out in back, while the party and its patrons raged on around me. He danced his way up to me with a gargantuan grin on his face, but then said nothing once he was near. One of the Kimpersonators threw a line at Marcus, "Twenty bucks for an hour, baby." Another pseudo-serious sentiment. It wasn't pure facetiousness; she'd been standing there silently for a few minutes and didn't use the line on me, but her attraction to Marcus compelled her to say something and she used the impervious cloak of irony to shield herself.

Marcus shut her down completely. "Sorry. I've only got some change and four cigarettes."

I'd consumed just enough booze to turn me a little socially brave, so I pulled out two fives and a ten and handed them over like a good tip at a shitty dive bar. She snatched up the money, stuffed the fives into her G-string and the ten into the piece of black polyester that covered her breasts; I saw her nipple as she did this and panicked anew.

Marcus got down in the societal gutter and said, "Sorry if this is presumptuous of me, but we really need to do the teeth-grab power-stripper move."

"We should at least be introduced first." She extended her bare arm to Marcus and said, "I'm Christina."

Marcus said his name through teeth clenched down on a five spot. I didn't introduce myself—it was only my money, not my teeth or tits—but when I saw one of the few girls who wasn't dressed slutty pull out her camera, I threw my head over Christina's shoulder and went for the ten like dumpster-diving behind the darkest porn store in town. It's all in the image. My beard must have hit her tits at some point.

"Oh my God, this is such an amazing picture," said Conservative Kim.

We left the money against Christina's body after we stopped posing. She reached down into her tits and pussy and pulled out the money. "Here, I guess you can have this back."

"I don't know if I want it back; it's been in dirty places," I said, but I reached out my open palm to show I was only joking, nervous about nearly licking her areola.

She shoved the money into my hand like it was a used condom, said, "Whatever," and stormed off like it was the morning after we'd had unsatisfactory, male-centric sex.

"I'm sorry. I was only joking," I said to her retreating backside as I lit a cigarette.

"Where are your pasties?" a Lil' Kim named Veronica said. She shined gaudily in a peach jumpsuit and gold chains.

"Sorry. I didn't have the chance to come over beforehand and get all dolled up," I said.

The week before she had flyered at yet another party I shouldn't have gone to and given me a speech, recited into cold-hard memory, about Kimdependence Day. I gave her that good ole social anxiety standby: "I'd love to come, but I don't have anything to wear."

"Even better," she'd said, "Or, come over early and we'll get you all whored up."

Today she said, "That's okay. There are other ways to show you're worthy of Lil' Kim."

"Like what?" I gasped; I was asphyxiated with aspartame and alcohol.

"Like dropping your pants."

I looked around and saw all the girls showing off their bodies, dressed in near-nothingness for the holiday. The boys were all fully clothed in tight jeans and sardonic hair-metal band T-shirts. The party was thick and murky with irony and slumming it for the night.

And then my cock was waving in the wind. Might as well go all out. Conservative Kim took her camera out again and I was twice immortalized in puerile stupidity.

Marcus glanced down at my genitals to see what all the hubbub was about, covered his eyes with his left hand—the one without a cigarette—and said, "Another line in appropriate social behavior crossed." This was drunk and socially sweat-soaked me, smashing through lines in acceptable behavior to remove focus from my lack of conversational skills.

Knowing that Marcus wouldn't come near me if my pants were around my ankles—he never does—I re-robed, grabbed his arm and pulled him onto me. With my arms around his waist I started gnawing his nipple through his shirt and screamed, "Where's the line at now?" He broke away from me, finished his cigarette in one long drag and went inside to slamdance my sleaziness away.

I lit another cigarette—barely finished with the previous—and eavesdropped on three different conversations at once without participating in a single one. The world had quickened its pace, but I was keeping up.

I was all alone when Christina came up to me and said, "I thought you were a prude or something and then everyone's inside talking about how the guy with the foot-long beard dropped trou in front of everyone. And I wasn't even here to see."

Everyone was talking about me; social aloofness was no longer a possibility. "If you want to see, I can do it again." I didn't care that my untrimmed bush nearly eclipsed my penis like the moon creeping over the sun in broad daylight, blocking the feature act. Though the sight of my cock, white as paint in the suburbs, wasn't nearly as magical as a solar eclipse.

"That's okay." Like a breathalyzer, she sensed the alcohol in my system, loosening my social restraints.

"That girl took a picture. You could just ask her."

"Why do you want to show everyone your penis?" Veronica asked. Where had she come from? Christina used this diversion to run back inside.

"It's Kimdependence Day," I said, clear as my empty cup.

"But I'm not running around showing off my twat."

"Pretty much." Earlier another girl had dropped a cigarette butt between Veronica's legs and dug it back out while everyone watched like a drive-in theater showing *Oil And Gold Diggers VIII*.

"Would you rather I didn't? Am I offending you?"

"What? I just thought if everyone else was doing it, I may as well get in on the action."

"How can you be so comfortable whipping it out like that?" she asked, like there was some inherent difference between cock and cunt.

"How's it a big deal?"

"I suppose it wouldn't be, for you, in front of a bunch of girls, huh?"

"What does that mean?"

"Big, overly manly beard on a scrawny white dude, licking

Marcus's nipples, comfortably showing your cock to a bunch of girls ... "

"Are you implying I'm gay? I'm not nearly as gay as I wish I was."

"How straight are you then?"

"I don't know ... eighty percent?"

"Prove it. Follow me."

Was she taking me to a roomful of hot, naked men and pulling my pants down to see if I became aroused? I didn't know, but I followed. Might as well go all out.

She took me into a bedroom and closed the door.

"Prove it."

"What do you want me to do?"

"Make out with me." She didn't consider that if I was straight I might not be attracted to her, which I wasn't all that much, or that if I was gay I could make out with her all the same.

But I did make out with her. It was sleazy as mud wrestling. Random ho basically begging for my balls. Ashamed, but I couldn't help it; I got an erection and the throb against her leg told her I had passed the test.

When we stopped, I started giggling and smiling like she was my dream girl noticing me for the first time.

"Look at you; all tense and awkward. Just relax," she said, and we were making out again.

"Are you wearing a wig?" I asked when I ran my hand through her hair.

"Yeah, isn't it amazing?"

"It looks real." I resumed my awkward state.

"Your fists are clenched. Relax."

More making out. I must have calmed down sufficiently because when she pulled back she said, "Yeah. I think we could have some fun later if you want to stick around."

Knowing you're getting laid, regardless of with whom, always helps relieve party angst. I was on the dance floor. I don't dance. I recognize how uncoordinated I am and how painful my dancing is for those within a five-mile radius. I was dancing and it felt great, though I had to take an occasional break on the outskirts of the floor in my usual wallflower stance, hands in my back pockets, to gain my bearings, sense of self and breath.

While on one of these breaks, a bikini top landed on my shoulder. Immediately I looked to see where it came from, but unfortunately saw no exposed breasts. With no owner to return the bikini to, I figured I'd just throw it on the ground with the rest of the party garbage—empty plastic cups, used napkins, a couple unmatched shoes—but then I looked at it and saw its American flag print.

I love patriotic apparel. I cannot help it. It's not quite mockery, but it's not exactly serious either. Maybe it's a desire for the tacky in the life I live otherwise frivolously. I do not fully understand this compulsion. I own four actual American flags, an American flag-design tie, a belt buckle that prominently portrays my patriotism, a pair of suspenders with bald eagles blazing and a 2003 George W. Bush calendar I've taken apart and retaped together so all the pictures form one blanket across my kitchen wall. Whenever I see a flag flying in an interesting place I take its picture; I have an entire photo album devoted to these shots.

I tore off my hoody and T-shirt and draped the bikini over my shoulders. I could not figure out how to tie the straps, so it hung loosely off my sunken chest. I dive-bombed the dance floor and cleared out a three-foot radius for my exuberant moves.

I had to pee. The bathroom was locked, but the lovely resident Lil' Kims had a bookshelf for me to glance at and feign interest in while I waited. The selection included both the sarcastic (those books you pick up from church rummage sales with titles like *So Human An Animal*), the serious (the inexplicably hip *Geek Love*) and old college textbooks (the enthralling *Men, Women and Rape*). As I was losing interest in judging the residents based on their tastes, Christina saddled up beside me and asked if I was waiting for the bathroom. I offered her the opportunity to go first, but she declined and picked up a Dostoevsky book I'd never heard of. It's a testament to how drunk I was that I still don't remember the title.

"Have you ever read Dostoevsky?" she asked me.

"I have. *Crime and Punishment* three times and *Notes From Underground* too."

"I love *Crime and Punishment*."

The bathroom door opened and a girl in a normal, everyday T-shirt and jeans came out. "I sorta put the new roll on for you, but not really," she said.

As I crossed the toilet threshold, Christina called out, "I want to keep talking about books with you."

I peed, flushed, then put the seat down. I went to the

mirror and popped a pimple.

"I'll be waiting," I said to Christina as we passed each other.

When she came out I saw she still had Dostoevsky in her hand. There may be nothing sexier than a whore (possibly from a Dostoevsky novel) carrying one of Dostoevsky's books and coming towards you. "Have you read other Dostoevsky?"

"I loved his short stories."

"I've never read them."

"He captures what it is to be human so well. Like each time you have a dream it's not exactly linear, but it shows what's weighing down on your mind." She was making hand motions like she was flustered or on speed.

"Everything the characters do is so deliberate and painstaking, but it feels so fast. Like being alive."

"Have you read his short stories?"

"No." We were drunkenly dissecting Dostoevsky in our dainty little outfits.

"I really love them. Especially there, you can really see it."

"I'll check them out."

"And everything he writes ties together so well. I mean, Crime and Punishment is huge, but things that are briefly mentioned in the beginning come back in the end."

"I was just talking to someone about an author who does that. Who else does that?" I hadn't had that conversation. I was filling airspace until she started talking again.

She sorta shrugged and said, "Lots of writers do that."

"What else do you recommend? I'm starting to run out of authors to read."

She said someone and I realized I was never going to remember the name, so I stopped listening.

"Look, I have a confession to make. Earlier, when I was so awkward about the money from your boobs, it was because as you put the money down there I saw your nipple."

"So what? Big deal." She pulled both sides of her top down and let her tits out.

And of course, Veronica walked up then. "What's this?" she asked and started feeling up Christina.

"I'm actually more comfortable in this than in regular clothes," Christina said, apparently oblivious to the groping of her tits. "This is closer to naked, which is really just me."

"You like naked, huh? How about this naked?" and Veronica stuck her index finger between Christina's G-string and skin and pulled down, revealing a smooth surface of skin.

"Yeah, that's fine."

"How do you feel about beards? He and I are going to fuck tonight. Wanna join us?"

Aren't I supposed to be consulted about this first? I thought. Then: Holy shit. There is no way this could ever happen to me.

"I think I'm just going to go home."

"Now?" I was silent during this transaction. Veronica's hand remained against Christina. "Have another glass of wine first."

"I think I will," and she was gone like a good little drunk.

"I'm going to go mingle."

I read the first paragraph of Dostoevsky and decided to get one of his books the next time I was at the library.

There were only five cigarettes left; I came with almost two full packs. I had smoked or given away over an entire pack. Wow, I thought, but I lit another one.

"I think I'm ready to take off," Marcus said.

"Okay. I'm staying. Have a good night."

He left with a girl I hadn't noticed before. She was the hottest girl I'd ever seen him leave a party with.

"Oh my God, Chloe, get your ass up and answer your phone. I want to go home and am not going out on the street in this," Christina was talking into a phone.

"Wait. Chloe. I've met her before," and I realized the Conservative Kim with the picture of my cock in the breeze was a friend of a friend, met at another party I was drunk enough to barely remember. "Why do you need her?"

"Because my clothes are in her apartment next door. It's too dangerous to walk home in something this skimpy and it's really fucking cold." Her impersonation came up against the harsh reality of Oakland at night.

"You could always stay here," Veronica said. How was she always around at opportune moments?

"I want to go home."

"Maybe you can borrow some clothes." Veronica escorted Christina into her room.

Another cigarette later: "Everything's winding down. People are going home. Let's go to bed. I think you're really going to enjoy this."

When we got into her room she immediately started undressing. "Do you want me to keep the bikini on?" I asked. She answered by lifting the straps off my shoulders. She reached up to the top of her head and I snatched her arms down. "Leave the wig on."

She had a loft bed with a ladder as narrow as a stiletto and I was drunk, with an erection throwing off my balance. "Be careful," she said as she turned off the overhead light, opting for the mood of lamplight instead.

There was already a person in the bed. A girl. A naked girl. A naked girl named Christina.

"What are you doing here?" I was still halfway on the ladder.

"I decided to stay and get my clothes in the morning. Is that okay? I can go."

"No. You can stay. It's fine. Let's go all out."

I had no idea what to do with one girl, let alone two. But this was typical-guy paradise: Two girls, one full-bodied and breasts big as white sand dunes, the other tiny and petite. One shaved, the other hairy. One pierced and tattooed, the other something for Thanksgiving dinner with grandma. And they both wanted to fuck me.

Veronica initiated a blowjob. Christina sat on my face.

She had an entire cigar box packed full of different kinds of condoms and lubricants. I reached in at random and pulled out something studded and ribbed. "Are you sure you're ready for that?"

As ready as I'll ever be. I strapped it on.

Whenever I fuck someone for the first time I fuck way too hard and way too fast. Although there haven't been a lot of cases studied, it seems to be a prevalent trend. This time it worked for Veronica, who, anytime I tried to slow down to catch my smoker's breath, accused me of teasing her; I should've known she'd fuck forceful based on her come-on. So I fucked Veronica as hard as I could and fucked Christina gently, catching my wind while doing so.

It was fun. I don't know how else to explain it. It was a bit like being on vacation at Disneyland; fast and furious and you don't really know what's going on or if you're enjoying yourself, but you're sure you'll long for it after you get back home. Kinda like regular sex for me.

"What can we do to make you cum?" Veronica cooed like a porn starlet.

"Yeah," Christina echoed.

"What about you two?" I was too uptight and tense to allow myself the intimacy of orgasm.

"I've cum so many times already."

"Me too."

They both kinda moaned loudly once or twice, but never that heart-stopping-jerk-I-need-to-stop-now-or-I'll-fucking-die reaction I associate with orgasm.

"Both of you give me head together. One of you suck my balls."

"Who are you? You come off all awkward at first, but during sex you're so up front and so, so dirty."

"That's not dirty." I am not trashy. Not really. "I'm a sexually open person," at least as much as someone who almost never has sex can be. "Are you going to blow me or what?"

They both put their faces in my crotch.

It was like it was the next day and the fireworks show had relocated from the marina onto my body.

"Let me fuck your faces a bit. I won't be hard. It won't hurt; I swear."

"You can do whatever you want."

I wanted to thrust my hips along while all my nerve endings exploded.

But I had to pee. I wasn't going to cum.

"You can stop. Your mouths have to be getting tired."

"Kinda," Christina laid down next to me.

Veronica kept sucking.

Then she stopped. "Yeah. This is tiring. Are you going to cum?"

I could no longer form words. I hadn't cum, per se, but the feeling all up and down my body was like a centralized orgasm in each part; my thigh was cumming, my elbow was cumming, my eyelashes were cumming. "I ... ech ... really ... rubjorbdg ... drunk. I have to ... psbzxilch ... pee."

"Use the towel to cover up."

I crawled back down the ladder with none of my body parts functioning.

When I came back up Christina and Veronica were making out. I almost fell off the ladder. "If you really want me to cum, how about both of you kiss me all over while I masturbate?"

Their lips were everywhere all at once and the feeling I'd managed to shake off while I peed was back. I felt an orgasm coming. Anticipation. "I'm going to cum. Watch out," and Christina moved her face out of the danger zone. Veronica sucked down my semen.

She spit it back onto my chest and screamed, "Now you're tainted too, bitch," through white, white teeth.

I had been thinking about naked, shaved men, greased up

like pigs, sucking and fucking aboard the U.S.S. Teabag.

I cleaned up and we laid down, mostly on top of each other, still drunk and thereby comfortable. "Goodnight Veronica and Christina." Always a gentleman.

"Goodnight," they both said.

Neither of them used my name. "Do you even know what my name is?"

"Ummm ... Beard-o?"

"Everyone at the party loved your beard."

"Really? Thanks. But my name is ... "

"I'm sorry. I don't know."

"Raskolnikov?"

"You fucked me and now you expect me to know your name? Come on."

"Reasonable enough. It's Ricardo."

"Shut up."

"Really?"

"Because that would be awesome."

"It is Ricardo."

"Wow. I had a threesome with a dude named Ricardo and ... some other girl."

"Veronica," I added. "I know because that's my mom's name." Back down to my awkward self.

"Okay. Veronica."

"Christina."

"And Ricardo." Ricardo is not my name. May as well go all out.

Refining My Sense Of Humor

first published online at opiummagazine.com

I always hate coming here, but Nicole insists. Lord knows why. She doesn't even smoke that much now that we're together. We're at her friend Eric's house. Eric is the biggest pothead I've ever met. I get a contact high here whether he's been smoking or not. Correction: the room has billowed with smoke like a bong chamber every time I've been here.

There are seven of us sitting in the living room plastered with Bob Marley posters. A bong makes the rounds. I'm the only one abstaining. Someone's playing Gamecube. As far as I can tell, Gamecube is the video game equivalent of Cooler Ranch Doritos: only consumable by a pothead.

Every once in awhile, someone says some pointless nothing about drugs. Nicole's telling a story about when she was fourteen. Her parents made her get monthly drug tests after she was busted. The stipulation was, "If you're doing drugs, you move out."

I say, "Know what I was doing when I was fourteen?"

"What, Tina?"

"Playing with my Barbies." You can tell a joke doesn't work when a bunch of stoners don't even laugh. "No, really we were too poor to afford Barbies. I was being fucked up the ass by my stepdad."

The whole room collectively gasps and then falls silent. Someone stops in the middle of a bong rip.

"I don't have a stepdad," I say. Nicole bursts out laughing. I really love that bitch.

Carbohydrate Coma

first published in Phraseology

During my first coffee break at work today I sent her a text message that read, "I want caffeine. I want to sleep. I want sugar. I want to die. I want anything but to be at work. More than all these things, I want to climb into your bed, put my head against your bosom and feel the bliss that follows."

She replied, "Still sick?"

I've never been one to abbreviate my speech. I text soliloquies. "I am super tired and stressed. And a bit sick still. I slept maybe three hours last night. I don't know if I'll make it out alive."

Luckily, work wasn't too bad. Most of the office went out last night for a co-worker's birthday. I wasn't the only one giving a lackluster performance. We were a drained and drudged office. I drank so much coffee and didn't even get gutrot. This is not a good sign. I need to start cutting back.

I almost puked into my salad at lunch.

The afternoon was a bedroom wall the day after you move out.

I got home and started reading *Generation X* for the fourth time. I'll finish it right before I close my eyes for the night. It's summer and the days are long. I'm sensitive to light and can't sleep during the day.

Not that I can sleep at night, either. This is why I feel like a cat injected with adrenaline inside a glass box during a lab experiment.

Dag sets the car on fire. There's a knock at the door.

"Hi." She kisses me. She has a plastic bag in her hand.

"Hey. What're you doing here?"

"Go get in bed. I'm going to make you breakfast. Pancakes, hash browns, biscuits and gravy, and orange juice. Lay down. I'm going to load you up with so many carbs you'll have no choice but to fall into a coma."

I keep reading in bed. I breeze through the book like it's an eighth-grade assignment. Really what I'm paying attention to is the sound of my love; the sizzle of oil, the plop of a flipped pancake, the pop of an opened juice carton.

We eat together and let the dishes crash beside my bed. She wraps her arms around my overstuffed belly and I fall asleep.

The Microwave Burrito Incident

There was no reason for the boss-man to handle the microwave burrito incident differently, but he did. What I did that day was no worse than what I did every day—came in late, screamed obscenities at paying customers, smudged my makeup together in some semblance of a face, blared death metal out over the gas pumps—but this set something off in the boss-man.

He licked his lips like there was donut sugar on them, just like he does every time he opens his maw at me, and said, "Christ, were you trying to give everyone E. coli?" His eyes were trained at my chest. Simple, like a single shot to the back of the brain. Somehow, when he got the divine inspiration to chastise me, there wasn't an old lady buying watered-down coffee or some fatass kid buying candy-coated candy. But still, the aisles were packed tighter than my cigarettes.

I don't embarrass that easily, but the way this woman ogling the shrink-wrapped sandwiches scrutinized me with her pupils—bottomless in the fluorescent-tube lighting—forced me to cover my eyes with both hands and not come out until I could remember to breathe. I nearly needed a smoke break, which would've really pissed off the boss-man; he'd have been left alone with the fresh-faced children from the neighboring school who had just chimed the bell on the front door with their entrance. I managed to overcome my crimson expression and continued tending to the glucose gluttons. And then, like always, ten minutes later, there was nothing to do but drink free coffee and smoke stolen cigarettes until I could punch the clock right in its ugly dome.

It was one of these boredoms that got me into this mess to begin with. A coworker microwaved one of those Bomb Beef Burritos, I suppose with the intention of eating the sludge, but decided he couldn't win the digestive war, so he offered it to me. Guess he forgot I make it a habit to eat real food, not space-age mock-ups of what food used to taste like. The plasticky meat smell repulsed me so strongly that I picked the slab up and chucked it across the store towards the trash. Since I didn't play sports in high school, the burrito decided not to hit its mark, choosing instead to burst its juices onto the doors. It's not like I hit anyone. E. coli wasn't even an option. And I made my coworker clean it up right away.

I had no intention of going back to work the day after being scolded. I was going to allow myself a day to be hungover in bed reading Anaïs Nin and Gertrude Stein, but I was the court jester shackled to King Convenience for his enjoyment. I had to go: rent, bills, responsibility; all that adult bullshit.

The rush was over, so I didn't anticipate anything happening unless I brewed it myself, and after the microwave burrito incident I was afraid of being burned. Every once in a while someone in a disheveled suit burst through the doors, late for a business meeting, diving for the remainder of the coffee. The ones who came in after the rush were always the people I hoped would forget to tie their ties, so it'd get caught in the wheel well as they ran a red light. These were the people I would imagine snapping a stiletto unexpectedly while parking their SUV, causing them to accelerate right through their private parking space, across the lawn—well-kept by a Mexican who'd worked harder every day of his life than any of the suits—and finally, smashing through the cubicles, massacring the day's agenda.

I was sitting on my stool reading the newspaper, making a vague effort to keep up with the world that rendered me—like phoning your senile mother in the nursing home—half asleep, nose touching a photograph of some newly genetically modified cornstalk or two lofty assholes shaking hands over a soon-to-be-broken peace accord when I heard that timid little voice, "I'm really sorry about what happened to you yesterday."

"Huh?"

"With your boss. That was really mean."

I removed the paper from my line of vision and came eye to eye with an androgynous ball of early puberty from the school next door. He had pale hair; blond or red or brown and still had the baby fat he would lose after he grew hair in his armpits. He was German or Irish or English or some other Western European nationality—some vanilla country whose insatiable explorers settled in America and decided to fuck the Earth fruitless with eight kids apiece until we had an entire country of facial replicas. He was contributing to his growth-spurt by buying cheese-encrusted chips and a soda the size of his femur.

"Oh, it's okay, really. I mean, I think I'll manage through these terribly turbulent times." I wondered if kids that age understood sarcasm.

"Glad to hear it. What happened?"

"Nothing. I don't want to talk about it." And I didn't. I wasn't about to explain myself to some kid. Dealing with the customers, especially the males, was always a stabbing pain in my lower back. I guess because I have tits I'm supposed to be interested in spawning with anyone who clutches a cock in order to pee, but truthfully, I couldn't fucking care less.

"Oh, sorry I bothered you." He turned his head down to the grout.

His voice wasn't a squawking joke of a transition. It was already chiseled in adulthood, waiting for the rest of his body to catch up. He was stuck in an extremely vulnerable time. Everything that touched him was going to leave a lasting mark, like fingers on an oil painting. Each motion he made was interpreted by his peers for popularity, his parents for potential and his psychoanalyst for problems.

"Shouldn't you be in school or something?"

"Probably. Shouldn't you?"

"School is for suckers. I can't afford to waste my time and money learning nothing in order to get a degree and then a job. A job is a job. It doesn't matter what title you put in front of your name, you're still just a title if that's how you choose to define yourself."

"I can't afford to be in there." He motioned in the direction of the school. "I'll die if I'm not careful."

"Everyone dies." I didn't know his exact circumstances, but I understood. Puberty is Latin for, "the whole world is against me." I used to be the fat girl who wore black, ate sack lunches alone and spent dances with E.B. White in the bleachers. "What's your name?"

"Kevin. Yours?"

"It's on the nametag."

"Lucy, I should probably get back. I'm really not that bold. I'm just skipping tech ed." He waved behind his back while trying to pull the door when he should've pushed. He didn't pay for his junk. I wasn't about to get off my stool to chase him.

Two days later I saw him again. On my way to the bus stop after work I heard his voice boom over the others on the playground. He was arguing over a kickball play at home plate. After the altercation subsided, his team went to play the field. Fully prepared to experience some vague middle school nostalgia, I sat and watched. He saw me and came over to talk through the chain link, in defiance of the teachers attempting to gain the advantage in the battle of chaos versus adulthood.

"That was totally unfair." He had little sweat beads dripping off his bowl cut. There's a certain age at which you can no longer pull off one of those atrocities to humankind, and he was just barely on the good side. His hand shielded his eyes from the midday sunshine. The other was wrapped around his waist. "I can't believe these jerks. I hate this."

"At least it wasn't league play. Then you'd really have something to complain about."

"What?"

"You didn't pay for your shit the other day."

"I must've forgot. I don't have any money on me."

"Don't worry, I covered it. You owe me, though."

"I can pay you back."

"Money is meaningless. Only experience has value. Come with me. You can get out of here and I won't have to go to the movies alone."

"I don't know. I have school. It's like, a law, for me to be here. I could get arrested."

In naiveté or brilliance, I was convinced I needed to feel the purity of a kid again, and he needed to see that there was life after middle school. Then I'd have to explain that there's life after high school, too. Hell, life doesn't really begin until you've broken free of societal constraints. Mine hadn't started yet. "You won't get in trouble. You can pick the movie. Meet me up front." I turned and walked away without looking back.

When I next saw him he was wearing a blue baseball cap and his backpack was strapped over a solitary shoulder. "Planning on staying out for the rest of the day?"

"I don't want to ever be here again."

It was an awful lapse of judgment to allow him to choose. Like any teenage boy, he picked a movie full of mannequin men masturbating machine guns. I think I offended him by explaining why blowing up mountains and wearing leather pants had no place in film, but not so much that he wouldn't grab a bite to eat with me afterwards. He got a double burger with American cheese, further contributing to his membership in Generation XL. I ordered a veggie burger and fries, which he ate the majority of. A cup of black coffee for me and a strawberry shake for him.

"Aren't your parents going to wonder where you are?"

"If they were around. They're on vacation. I should get back soon. They call every few days."

His little nook of living was on the way to mine, so I offered to walk him. A real sweetheart. The night had become chilled. I loaned him the stocking cap I never wear but always keep in my coat's secret pocket. He pointed out that the sky looked like an inverse sunrise at night—there were no city lights over the lake to the East, which made the West much brighter in the dark. Everything was backward, but it was always as such. Usually I'm shut down in social situations, not willing to dish out my opinions to ingrates and morons, but Kevin kept me talking. From the most recent reality TV show results to his fear of snakes, from bowling alleys to classrooms, from light switches to hair metal, all bases were articulated. The ten blocks to his house were an airport terminal moving sidewalk, right on down to the emotional baggage.

I was so cold by the time we got to his house that I accepted his offer to warm up at the fireplace. His parents' house was absurd. Poor kid. The den was as big as my entire apartment, with dead trophies and giant bookshelves lined with musty encyclopedias with uncracked spines. The fireplace ignited with the push of a button. I attempted to sit in the huge leather chair next to the fireplace, but he said, "That's my dad's. He doesn't like anyone else in it." Since his dad was so particular about his ass groove, I was relegated to the couch. He could've sat on the loveseat across the mahogany table from me, but opted to sit next to me, practically on top of me, instead. The social fluidity I had witnessed on our walk was poured down the sink. He was nervous now, bouncing his leg up and down and scouring his palms against his thighs. When he said anything, he stumbled over his words, each syllable a pilgrimage to failure.

Maybe he thought he owed me for pulling him out of class. Maybe for the movie or his chips and soda. He lifted his head and kissed me. I put down my shield and ran with it. What the fuck else was I going to do? That night, on his parent's couch, next to an almost-fire, I opened my drawbridge and let him across with full diplomatic immunity.

Immediately, he made it known that he was a warring nation, awkward throughout the attack. At times I thought my spleen would vent through my back beneath his bulk. He devoured me like I was on the dollar menu. I was fucking toxic waste waiting to be shoved into barrels and lined in concrete. He smelled heavily of cheap, powdery deodorant. The sex was awful, but the way he squeezed his eyes—his eyelids were jewel-encrusted knives in their sheaths waiting to be pulled—made it worthwhile. It was over almost as soon as it started.

I lay, being gawked at like a beached whale, breathing smoke and looking at the ceiling fan when he bombed me. "Do you want to stay here tonight?" The troops had gone out to get drunk and laid. My base was left vulnerable not just to invasion, but to occupation.

"I need to get home. I'll see you around." I walked into the still of three a.m.

It wasn't guilt. The mother who isn't qualified to teach but still homeschools her kid to protect him from bullies doesn't feel guilty. I searched for something to be upset with myself about, but found nothing. He was an adolescent boy; of course he wanted it. Still, there was something nagging at me, something indoctrinated by a corrupt society. And there was its physical manifestation on the curb in front of the store the next day. "Shouldn't you be in school?"

"I told you I quit."

"I've got to work."

"See you when you're done."

When I finally assumed my position behind the register, he was still on the curb, sitting there like a scar to remind me of what happened. With eyes averted from each passing customer, he paced and paced and paced the sidewalk. If the boss-man had noticed, Kevin would've been eighty-sixed for loitering, or, better put, "This is a market economy and I'll be goddamned if you get to sit around on your ass while I toil away needlessly." At least he climbed the fence to be with his classmates when they came out for recess. He wasn't a total teenage stalker, looking to fill some void with an exotic older woman—he just didn't know what else to do or where else to be. He was lost. He needed help. He turned to me.

While the boss-man was occupied with some blue-haired woman in rollers counting pennies for her loaf of fluffy white bread, I escaped out the back door and pushed Kevin into the car parked in front of him. "What's up?"

"My day's pretty boring without school."

"Yeah, that's why I have a job."

"Maybe I should get a job."

"You're too young for that shit. Get back in school."

"I don't like it."

It was hard to argue with that. "Want to get some ice cream?" Even I knew how to make my digestive tract run the gauntlet once in a while.

His face lit up like a child's. "Let's go to Custer's."

Custer's was a theme restaurant. Some fucking genius who flew through business school on Gold Card wings imagined General George Custer and ice cream belonged together. They took all the plastic war replications they could get their hands on, threw them under a flat pale roof on a pale concrete building and turned the volume up to full. The wretchedness of children abandoned with babysitters for the day was used as kindling in the hate-fire. A putrid plastic tube with a pinball bouncing inside ran throughout the restaurant. The ball brought with it the rewritten history of Custer's failing bugle call by knocking over these little cardboard Native stereotypes like college sports mascots. They somehow managed to make Custer out to be not only victorious, but just. The menu consisted of those good old Midwestern meals—hamburgers extra red, fried cheese curds and ice cream topped to the sky with fudge and nuts. There was no hint at something as blasphemous as a salad bar. Fitting that the genocidal raping of the Natives was attached to the slaughterhouse raping of cows. "If I fucking go there you will be cleaning my brains off the booth before our order arrives." He missed the joke. There was an element of truth, but I wouldn't kill myself over a restaurant; the restaurant would kill me. "Never mind. I don't want any ice cream. Let's take a walk."

We ended up at a secluded spot on Lake Michigan. I don't know how it existed. Like the few cultures that haven't been touched below the belt by Catholic missionaries, it remained in its unexplored schoolboy state. It wasn't some mystical spot unscathed by human interaction where you could go and have a Thoreauvian religious experience, but it was away from all those magazine cover girls who overpopulate most beaches. The green-brown seaweed crawled up there on the shore, pleading to die, clutching its last revenge against the world in the stench it feebly threw out at upturned noses.

We sat on a rock washed flat by years of high tides. Each time he tried to prod the silence, I hit him flat-palmed in the back of the head. I wanted to inhale the death of the city that suburbanites got to breathe daily. He wanted to convince himself he was a part of my existence. Once he learned to shut up and behold his surroundings, I held him between my arms and legs. Four eyes looked out across a lake without a horizon.

He kept fucking turning around to look at me, though. Those beady little green shitballs were expecting something from me. They were begging me. I tried looking longingly and deeply into his pupils, but only started laughing at the romantic comedy. I tried looking the other way, but his body refused to turn around and ignore mine. I tried slapping his pudgy cheek, but couldn't bring myself to do it with any real violence. I tried kissing him, but the seagulls were watching and would call out my crime each time. No matter what, his little eyeballs stayed trained on me. I was being vacuum sealed and made ready for a freezer I wasn't yet prepared to rot in. I got off the rock and walked back toward civilization.

I was halfway up the hill before he yelled, "Hey! What's going on?"

"I'm leaving."

"Should I come with?"

"Do whatever the fuck you want."

He didn't follow me.

The Note

First, I'll admit I parked kinda dunderheadedly last night. I was lit. Gin. It's so dark out here where there are no streetlights. The sort of darkness where it seems like light is afraid to come out. I don't think I'll ever get used to this darkness.

Even last night I knew I'd have to come back and fix it. Nothing I could do about it then.

Eight hours later, I stagger out in my wife's robe to grab the paper. Some guy in plaid is bent into the cab of an enormous pickup, stopped in the middle of the road. The engine runs at a roaring idle. Behind him, no shit, a pack of wild turkeys is gathered. Too weird, I think, too hungover. In order to return balance to the world, I need to move my car. As I'm releasing the emergency brake, I hear, "Nice fucking park job, buddy." I slowly ease past his beast-truck. He throws something at me. Direct blow to my addled head. A note so reproachful and self-righteous I forgo the paper and read it aloud to my wife while we lick syrup from our fingers.

"It isn't hard to park. I don't understand what the problem is for you. There is so much space here. Not everyone drives a miniature-sized car. I need space to fit through. Not like you had to parallel into a tiny spot in the city. No. Out here, we don't do this sort of thing." I repeat this line: "Out here, we don't do this sort of thing. There was no one else around and you couldn't manage. Idiot. It's really very simple. You're halfway out into the road on a corner. You're going to kill someone. You idiot."

All is well with the world again.

Slow Roast

There wasn't so much as a particle of precipitation in the pallidness that pretended to be air that summer. August in the year of the drought, when all the plants shriveled up like ash, when the public pool closed down because water that would have been overchlorinated was instead overpesticided and irrigated to fields to sustain some semblance of sorghum. The desert had skipped town—it was sick of the Southwest—and moved into my subdivision, becoming my new Nebraskan neighbor, knocking on the front door and asking to borrow a cup of sugar to make some lemonade so it could just maybe stave off this heat for a minute or two. Going outside felt like dehydration personified, so when my dad told me he thought it was time for me to get a part-time job, I cracked up like the sun-baked earth. Slow roast, 120°F for a hundred hours.

"Son," he said, sounding like a video I'd watched the year before in health class, "You're thirteen years old now. That's a big age. You're a teenager. Soon enough you'll be an adult, and with that comes a lot of freedom. I think you need to take on more responsibility so you'll really appreciate that freedom."

I paused my video game. "What kind of responsibility?"

He rattled the ice in his whiskey and water. "You're getting a part-time job. When I went through the Burger Barn Drive-Thru for lunch today, I noticed the marquee said they were hiring."

I started shooting villains and saving the world again.

"Excuse me, but I'm talking to you."

"I'm listening."

"Please turn off the game."

"Why?" Level up.

"So we can talk about this."

"We're already talking."

"Edward, turn that game off immediately."

If I could just get up to that platform then I could reach the pendulum and ... "Hey! Why'd you turn my game off?"

"I picked up an application for you. Fill it out and give it back to me. I'll turn it in. And Edward, do a good job."

"Dad. It's a hundred and ten degrees outside. Remember when you said if school had started yet, it'd be canceled? And now you want me to get a job? And not just any job, but a job at Burger Barn, which is probably the hottest place in town? No way."

The heat poached this crazy bravado out of me. "Can we turn the air conditioner up?"

"No, we cannot. The fact that you're so resistant to this shows me you need it."

"I'd resist getting beaten up, and I don't need that."

"This is different. Here's the application and a pen. Get to work."

He went outside through a screen door expanded and sticking in the heat. He thought if he didn't smoke in front of me it wouldn't make as much of an impression on my fragile little mind. I turned my game back on and refilled my AK-47.

The boss had less life than a dog left in a car with the windows rolled up, but that didn't stop my dad from hitting the power button again. "You could at least let me save my game first."

"How's that application coming?"

"I'm thinking about it. I need to make sure I do my best if I want to get the job."

"Have you even looked at it yet?"

"Of course I have."

"Name any question on it."

"Ummm ... " I stared at the blue video screen, looking for an answer. "Why do I want the job?"

"Do you need me to sit here and help you?"

"I'll do it."

"By tomorrow. When I go to work in the morning, I want to drop this thing off."

"Okay."

"Got it?"

"Yeah, yeah. I got it."

"Edward, where is that application?"

I dropped my spoon into my cereal, reached in my pocket and pulled out the end of my freedom. The sugar slopping continued.

Dad pulled his English muffin out of the toaster—normally he was a bacon-and-eggs man, but it was too hot to cook up some coagulation of the arteries—and spread the strawberry jam. "This is folded. You can't hand in a folded-up application."

"Sorry. I didn't know." The news was on; another scorcher of a day, no sign of letting up.

"It's obvious. You're trying to make a good impression. You don't want them to know you're a pig."

"I didn't think it was a big deal. Look, I'm sorry."

"I can't turn this in."

"So don't, then."

"You'd like that, wouldn't you?" He put the jam back in the refrigerator and the door closed with a pop louder than necessary.

"I don't want a job. Especially not at Burger Barn."

"You're getting a job. If you screw this one up, then we'll keep trying."

"None of my friends have jobs."

"They will soon enough. You'll be the first one to jump on this bandwagon."

"But Dad! Burger Barn! Everyone'll make fun of me."

"Do you know what my first job was? I cleaned rooms at a hotel. A job now only suited for Mexicans. It doesn't get any lower than that. It'll do you some good to be demeaned."

I got up and put my spoon and bowl in the dishwasher. "How so?"

"I don't have time for this. I have to go to work. I'll get a new application and fill it out for you. Try to do something besides play video games all day. I'll see you when I get home."

His car keys jangled like an oven timer. I dragged myself into the living room to happily while away in front of the big-screen TV.

"Is that what you're wearing to your interview?"

"I'd planned on it."

"You're wearing jeans. They don't even allow you to wear

32

jeans when you're working. Go put on some khakis."

"Is the shirt good enough for you?"

"It's fine, just button the top button."

I broke into a sweat trudging up and down the stairs. "I'm going to get sweat stains just biking the six blocks there."

"Put on some more deodorant, leave early and take breaks every couple blocks. Take a water bottle."

"Every couple blocks? It'll take me half an hour to get there. Can't you give me a ride?"

"I can't do the job for you. What're you going to do when I'm working? You'll still have to get there then, so you may as well figure out how to do this without stinking now."

Really, he wouldn't give me a ride because he couldn't drive without a cigarette in his hand. "I should get going then."

"Goodbye."

I tentatively touched the doorknob to test for fires. "Hey Dad, when you rewrote my application you didn't change anything, did you?"

"Why?"

"Just making sure I don't have to lie or anything."

"I would never ask you to do that."

"Bye."

"Hey Edward, good luck."

He followed me outside to smoke. He even smoked outside when I wasn't around so the smell wouldn't seep into the sofa and tempt me with its stale acridity.

Drought day 1,027. Or at least it felt like it. How do you keep track of days when you spend all your time waiting for night, waiting for the redemption of heat without the blare and blast of sunshine? It was too hot to eat, so for breakfast we were melting ice cubes in our palms, on our foreheads and chests. "Still haven't heard back from Burger Barn?"

The word "no" cracked out of my throat, like walking through the barrenness of the sandy deserts of Mars without an oxygen mask.

"It's been a week. You sure the interview went okay?"

"It seemed okay to me, but I've never done one before, so who knows. It's too hot to work, anyways."

"Speak for yourself." Dad put his shirt on, which immediately clung to the sweat on his skin like a divining rod. "Someone around here has to keep us stocked up on ice, to pay the electric bill so the air conditioner can run. I have to go to work."

"Good luck with that."

How many drinks was that? I lost count. I knew it had to be at least four, so I'd be okay. I was shooting for six before I told him, but he was done drinking and on his way to sleep. Or at least to lie in bed, roll around, and try not to drown in any sweat pools.

"Dad?"

"Yeah, Eddie?"

He was drunk alright. He usually started calling me Eddie after five drinks. Maybe tonight's were a bit stronger than usual, designed to douse the fire in his belly—everywhere—that comes with the ever-reliable readings of temperatures so exponentially high. "Burger Barn called today."

"And?" He swaggered in anticipation.

"I got the job. I start tomorrow."

"Oh, great. That's just great, Eddie-boy. Congratulations."

"Yeah, thanks."

I watched TV for fifteen more minutes; just enough time for him to pass out before I started rummaging through drawers like a woodpecker poking his beak into a saguaro, looking for water. His spare pack of cigarettes was jammed between the sandwich bags and the aluminum foil. I grabbed one, along with the book of matches and went outside.

I was never much into fireworks or even melting action figures in the microwave, but the air was dead, windless, and I lit my first cigarette with the first match I'd ever struck. It tasted like suicide, like forgetting to put sunscreen on before going outside, like a firefighter coming with a wrench and turning off the hydrant you've been playing in.

It was exactly what I wanted.

Halfway through, I started to feel light, like rising, like mercury. By the end, I felt I knew what death was really like. I tossed the stump onto the ground and floated into the backyard to see if there was any grass left to lie in. When I found there was nothing but brittle dirt as dry as the public pool, I turned around to go back inside.

The house was on fire. Half of it was no longer a house, but a fireball; the half where I'd smoked, the half where my dad's bedroom was.

I just stood there and watched it—him—burn. It never occurred to me to get help or to rush in there and pull Dad out. It never even occurred to me that I was doing the wrong thing, just standing there. I wasn't helpless or helpful, I just was. I was transfixed by the fire like a kid playing a video game. I didn't move until a firefighter saw me and escorted me into an ambulance.

I didn't go to work the next day.

This Is So Boring I Need Drugs

My little brother handed me the telephone. "Guess who it is," he said like the sarcastic little twit he was.

His sarcasm got the point across. I instantly knew it was my friend Lucas, who was close to the only person to ever call me.

"Jesus," I said into the phone, "Don't you have any other friends?" I may have taught my brother how to be sarcastic.

"Not really. Does that make me a loser?"

"Me as your only friend? Huge loser."

A moan of dejection like the sound a motorcycle makes when it sputters to a stop. "I may as well kill myself then."

"How're you going to do it this time?"

"My dad just got in a shipment of fertilizer. Not even opened yet. I figure I jump in the box, reseal it and before I can even ask why, I'll be suffocating in methane."

"Drowned in farts. I give it three bullets."

"Only three? Dude! Imagine that smell. That's a gross way to go. You'd have to be pretty sick to torture yourself that way."

"I suppose it's at least worse than slitting your wrists."

"At least? Dude, way worse!"

"I don't know. It's got spirit, but it lacks spunk. No heart. No blood even."

"This judging is rigged. I'm going to beat you."

"I'll see you in about half an hour then."

"I'm going to shower and eat first."

"Okay. Later." I turned the TV off mute and popped a cheese-encrusted snack into my mouth.

The family's Maltese started barking like Jesus had risen from the dead.

"Chill out. It's just Lucas." I unlocked the door to find Lucas wearing the same uniform as always—sunglasses, blue workshirt, green cargo pants, flaps of canvas on his feet hardly worthy of being called shoes and a caffeine-filled soda.

"What's up man?" I said.

"You know, nothing. You?"

"Old SNL episodes. That's about it."

"Well, alright then."

We sat in silence while watching one of Chevy Chase's finer pratfalls.

Lucas spoke. "What's going on tonight? You talked to anyone?"

My eyes stayed trained on the TV. "Beth, Susan and Tanya might go to Alton."

"Eeeww. For boys?"

"I imagine so." I rolled my eyes.

"Got any ideas?"

I let the TV gloss over my eyes. "Nope. They might not go. Wanna see what we can find in the meantime?"

"Can't we just call someone?"

"You know that never works."

"I know."

"Well?"

"Alright. Let's go."

I went into my parent's bedroom, a dull shade of seafoam green, and found them lying in their waterbed watching some cheap action flick. "Lucas and I are going out."

"Take a phone." It didn't matter which one said it. Nor did it matter which of their phones I took. It didn't really matter if I grabbed a phone at all. No one would call.

Up and down. Block to block. Down and up. The same path. Over. Over. Over and over. Accelerate. Blinker. Brake. Turn. Accelerate. Blinker. Brake.

"This is terrible. It's still too early for people to be out."

"You might be right. Let's get food."

He got a bag of licorice. I got a shrink-wrapped ham sandwich. We sat in the parking lot, eating and brainstorming.

"We could always call Frank and Morey."

"Yeah, but I really don't want to. We always end up with

them. And it's always the same."

"What about Jeremy?"

"I don't know. There's always Kelly." Somehow Kelly had infiltrated our circle of acquaintances—friends—and no one seemed to question it besides us.

He didn't laugh. I didn't know if he understood that I was joking. "Seriously. Not funny. Let's go to Jeremy's.

Accelerate. Blinker. Brake. Accelerate. Brake.

"Turn around! That was Jared and Amy."

"Where?" Even if he didn't see the couple himself, he trusted my vision and turned the car around. "How do we stop them?"

I pushed the button to roll down the window—slow as everything in this town—and stuck half my body out, flailing arms and straining vocal cords to get noticed. They turned left at the stop sign and we lost them in traffic. How did that little town ever create traffic?

"We should've taken my car. I hate automatic windows."

"At least this has a CD player."

"Shut up, you son of a pogo-stick."

"Oh that's it. I'm tyrannosaurusing all over your ass."

I turned my butt toward him and said, "Bring it, baby," in my most seductive voice.

"I'm not doing that again."

We lost ourselves in laughter.

"To Jeremy's then?"

I nodded in approval. He turned the car around.

Accelerate. Brake.

"It doesn't look like he's here."

"Doesn't he usually work Friday nights?"

"I think so." I had no idea. I didn't even know what he did for a job. Probably bussed tables. About all that could be done in a town that barren of business.

We rarely hung out with Jeremy, but he was usually the first one on our list of possibilities. When we did hang out, it was a good time. The kid had an air of awesomeness. Like hanging out with a sea lion.

"Might as well keep going then."

Accelerate. Brake. Accelerate. Brake.

"What's up?"

"Just driving around. You?"

"Thinking about getting going on my AP Lit paper." We had seen Casey's car in his driveway and figured we may as well stop.

"Seriously? Weak. It's Friday. Do you know what Friday means?"

"What're you guys doing that's so much better?"

"At least we're trying."

"You're not doing a very good job. Call me if you find anything to do tomorrow night. Later."

Tomorrow night? The same, no doubt.

"Let's go by Morey's." I couldn't believe I had suggested it.

"At least it's by the park. And Jane's. Maybe something else is going on there."

"Right. Exactly." I acted like my intention hadn't been as defeatist in nature as seeing if Morey was home.

"Do you see that?" We had driven into a cornucopia of communal activity—a semi-ironic four-square game. The tennis court had been chalked off and in the box stood Alex, Jared, Amy and Sam. Jane, Karen, Pat, Kyle, Wes and Jeremy all waited in line.

Lucas parked the car and we both got out yelling. "Now the game has begun."

"Get ready for cremation."

"Straight underground, yo."

"Like ex-presidents."

"Word."

We couldn't get enough of making asses of ourselves.

"We just called last play."

"What're you up to next?"

"I don't feel well," Jared said.

"I want to be alone tonight," Alex said.

"I think I'm going to go home and watch *Sixteen Candles*," Jane said with eyes wide.

I rolled my eyes and asked how many times she had already seen it.

"I don't know. Does it matter? Girls' Night! Anyone in?"

You have got to be kidding me, I thought. But all females affirmed that they were indeed in. Actually at that point, even *Sixteen Candles* sounded reasonably fun, but that might have been because I wasn't invited.

That left me, Lucas, Pat, Kyle, Wes and Jeremy.

"Alright, fellas. The six of us. What's up?" Wes had the rubber ball cradled in his right arm.

"Freestyle session!" Pat yelled and slapped the chainlink engulfing the court.

"What?" Lucas was as perplexed as I was.

"We had a bit of a freestyle earlier," Jeremy started.

"And it was awesome," Pat finished.

"I'm standing hereonthis logand I look   just like afrog. Eating a peanutbutter sandwich and thanking Mom it ain't Manwich."

Lucas and I made desperate eye contact. "I think we're going to be taking off then."

Our pace seemed to be slower than before. "This is so boring I need drugs. Stop at the gas station." Lucas obliged and I got us each a dose of soda.

Accelerate.

"This town is stupid. Four thousand people and no one wants to do anything."

"Most of that four thousand is cows," I corrected him.

"I can't wait to get out of here."

"We need to move."

"We need to finish high school."

"I need to pass geometry."

"Easy enough if you care."

"I need to care then."

"It's not worth it. Geometry isn't going to make life any more interesting." He was younger than me by a year but didn't act like it.

"You're right."

"We should burn this whole town to the ground."

"Pastures and all."

"And let's not forget the boredom."

"Can boredom be burned?"

"I don't know, probably."

"Or we could just get a movie."

"And go where to watch it?"

"My house, I guess. As long as we're quiet. My mom made cookies today."

"To the video store."

Turn. Brake.

"Isn't that your neighbor?"

"Yeah. Maybe we can get a free movie out of him."

"Hey Justin. What's up?"

"Just getting a movie."

"Oh yeah? Which one?"

He held up a case I hadn't seen before.

"I haven't seen that yet." I couldn't believe it. I thought Lucas had seen everything. He was a connoisseur of boredom, of two-hour long fillings, of movies. "Wanna watch it with us?"

"I need to watch at home. I'm waiting for Laura to call."

I wasn't sure who Laura was, but let it be. There was nothing left in the store that interested Lucas and me.

Back to the road. Pavement. Sidewalk. Lawn. Gnomes. Accelerate. Brake.

"Isn't that Michelle's car? Let's stop."

My atrophied wrists pounded at the door as hard as they could.

The seal of door and frame was broken by a woman I assumed to be Michelle's mom.

"Hi. Is Michelle around?" Lucas spoke. Adults made me nervous. Cramped up.

"She isn't here and won't be back tonight." She closed the door and pushed out a puff of air that smelled miraculously like Michelle.

"Tonight has been so lame."

"There's still Frank and Morey." I hated the suggestion, but it was all that remained.

"You're right. Let's go."

Accelerate.

"We were just wondering when you guys would show up." Frank smiled at Morey.

"You always do." Morey pumped a fist.

"Yeah, we do." I didn't hear disappointment in Lucas's voice, more like the calm acceptance of fate, like a captain realizing his ship is sinking.

"We knew it would be soon, so we had this waiting for you."

Morey pointed to the table. His first name was Joe, but everyone called him by his last name.

"Didn't see that coming." I rolled my eyes, but I doubt anyone saw through the dark.

"Spark it up, man. Honor's yours."

Always the modest one, Lucas said, "You sure?" but was already moving his hands toward the table.

"I'm sure." Frank handed Lucas the pipe and a purple lighter. Flick. Lucas handed them to me. Flick. I handed them to Frank. Flick. Frank handed them to Morey. Flick. Morey handed them to Lucas.

Flick. Inhale. Hold. Exhale. Pass. Flick. Inhale. Hold. Exhale. Cough. Pass. Flick. Flick. Flick. Pass. Pass. Flick. Inhale.

"There's nothing on TV, man."

"This thing is so stupid."

"So am I right now."

"Me too."

"Totally."

We all agreed.

"Know what we should do? Smoke another one!" Morey always wanted another, no matter what portion of the Earth's atmosphere he was in.

"I can't."

"Me neither. I'm ready for bed. And I've gotta drive home still."

"Wanna take me home?" I could barely keep my eyes open they were so dry. In need of eyedrops or complete and total isolation.

Ac ce le rate . Br   ake. B rak e.Brake. Tur n. Accele r a t e . T urn. B r a k e .

Not The Event, But Certainly An Event, Which Led To My Current Alcoholism

We knew about the campsite through some sort of teenage folklore, passed down through generations of kids who needed breaks from their parents and school. We trekked back a softly muddy, narrow path. Thick pine needles slapped our faces as we towed forbidden coolers. Just when I was beginning to break a sweat, we reached total seclusion: a cliff off the back and dense forest surrounding. The nighttime was black.

Prompt as a school bell, we cracked open beer cans and took off our shirts.

We were young and teeming with hormones "We need girls," my friend with the precipice of a mustache said. Magically, like the alcohol, girls appeared. They got drunk.

Through alcohol and skinny dipping we explored others' bodies, our own bodies.

My susceptibility to peer pressure was best evidenced by my becoming more inebriated than ever before in my short life. So when my friends told me how hot these girls I'd never thought of before were, I believed them. Suddenly my friends' rambunctious randiness made sense.

And then everyone disappeared, bodies stacked on bodies in tents, heaving silhouettes revealing their intentions. I offered Heidi Pitts, somehow still outside with me, a beer, and before I could open it we were under a picnic table, the last place on Earth, my hand against the wire of her bra.

"Wait," she said, pressing the abundance of my face flesh back in restraint. "Tell me I'm pretty."

Pretty or not wasn't something I'd considered. I thought about this and then I mumbled back, like speaking through a stretched rubber band, "You have a nice face, but you could use a new body," oblivious to my own heaving bosoms.

After she ran away crying, I could only get drunker, alone and drunk enough to throw firewood at approaching hungry raccoons.

Reconnect

My phone rang in the middle of the night, waking me up in a panic. It vibrated underneath its factory-installed tone. Those vibrations compounded my panic. The ID box said Angela. It took me a second to remember who Angela was. I had edited her name from Parakeet. I didn't want to lose her, but she couldn't stay the same. "Hello," I answered with a voice like sanding a frog.

She waited. It could have been trepidation. "Hi," was all she said. Like that was all that was necessary.

I didn't know what to say. I asked how she was. Fine, she said, good even, and asked about me. I told her I was alright. No need to say more than that, not yet. It should have been her turn to talk; she called me. She didn't say anything. I waited before I asked her how she'd been.

"Okay. Up and down. You know how it is. You?"

"Some of the same. More downs than ups, but okay. Ultimately."

Neither of us spoke for a bit. I was waiting, desperate and hopeful, to learn the reason she called. It didn't seem like she would go on. "Why are you calling?" I put too much emphasis on the why, like I didn't want her calling me at three in the morning, like it was a hindrance and not a godsend.

"I wanted to check up on you. Make sure you're okay."

"At three in the morning?"

"Okay." I heard her staticky exhale on the other end. "I miss you."

"Really?"

"I'd like to see you again."

"We should get together sometime." Now, I wanted to say.

"Now. If we don't do this now I'll never have the courage to do it. Now. Please."

"You're drunk." She was slurring. I had my doubts she'd remember calling me come morning. "If we're going to do this, we're going to do it right."

"Please. Now," sobbing. That was exactly how I remembered her voice.

"No. You'll regret it in the morning and hate me even more. I won't do it."

"When then?"

"How drunk are you?" The abruptness of my question jolted me even. "Are you going to be able to leave your house tomorrow night?" I softened.

"Yeah, that should be fine."

"Good. Let's get some drinks at Lenny's then."

"What?" She snapped like a baseball hitting a mitt.

"Kidding. Only a joke."

"Not funny."

She was right. Way too close to home. "It's the middle of the night. Give me a break. We'll get dinner. Coach at eight?"

"I'll be there."

"Good." No one spoke. Then, "I'm really excited to see you," I said.

"Yeah. Tomorrow then. Bye."

I didn't know how to fall back to sleep. I wouldn't, I was sure of it. Another night of fitful sleeplessness, imagining the possibilities, playing out conversations in my head, trying to figure out how I could make everything better. The next day had to be perfect. I needed to fine-tune each and every syllable. My dialogue was revised at least a hundred times. I didn't deserve a chance, but thanks to the good side of alcohol I had one. I could not afford to screw this up any more than I already had.

I was sitting down inside, waiting. I didn't want to come in, didn't want to put my anxiety on display for the waitstaff, but I couldn't face the desperation of waiting in the barren parking lot either. She was late. Only a couple minutes, I reminded myself. Not like her to be late, though. Or, hadn't been like her. Maybe she'd changed. I sure have, I told myself.

She's decided against coming, I thought. Can't say I blame her. I wish she'd show up. I just want to explain it all to her. I want to apologize some more. I owe her that much. I want everything to go back to normal. Move past it like nothing ever happened.

"Look at you. You look great." I had been staring into the sprawling whiteness of my napkin and she snuck up on me.

"Thanks," I stood. I even wore a tie. I pulled out the chair opposite me. "I thought you weren't going to show up."

"I wasn't. I thought about it at least. How are you?"

"Scared, nervous, so happy you're here. You?"

"God. What a question. I don't know."

We both sipped from our water glasses. Together. The service was good. Already, the waitress was over my shoulder asking about drinks and appetizers. We declined both.

I had so much to say. I didn't want to be the one to initiate talking. I didn't want to push myself on her. "You really look beautiful. I always loved that dress."

"Thanks." She wore her long-flowing white dress. No straps. Real casual, but elegant, like a wedding cake. She knew I loved it.

We sat in silence. That silence was like when you see the doctor coming to the waiting room to give you the prognosis. The space between lighting the fuse and the explosion. The dead air space after the first time you tell someone you love them.

"It's been hard for me without you."

I didn't deserve to hear that sort of tenderness from her. "Why?"

"You were such a huge part of my life that's just not there anymore. The adjustment. I don't know. I miss you."

Those words like honey dripping from a bumblebee's stinger. "I miss you, too."

"I figured you'd be happy and moved on by now."

"It'll be a long time before I'm able to let someone else into my life."

She shot me a look that could shatter glass. I took a sip of water and decided to hold back. "Not like that. I meant emotionally."

"I know what you meant."

"I'm sorry."

The waitress came back. Coach was the real deal. White button-down shirt with the sleeves rolled up. Little black pleated skirt those women put on just for me to enjoy. Hair up in a bun. An actual pad of paper to scribble our order down. We came here for our six-month anniversary. I chose it because it was far enough back in our past that our memories could be hopeful without being painful. We both ordered ribeyes, hers bloody enough that she should have had to sign a waiver and mine crispy enough that it may no longer have been meat. Potatoes on the side. No dessert yet, wait and see.

"Still at the same job then?"

"Yeah. I know, I know. You?"

"Yeah."

"Seeing anyone?" I didn't want to ask.

"Do you think I'd be here if I was?"

"Maybe. I don't know."

"You don't get it, do you?"

"Get what?"

Her eyes followed our waitress. She had a tray too full of food to be ours. Angela watched her anyways. She ever so slightly puckered her lips, like thinking of lemonade. She did this whenever she was deep in thought. I let my question go.

"I always feel so good when I'm with you. I don't know. You made me feel like everything was going to be okay. Even now. I still feel that way and I hate it."

"I'm sorry."

"Will you quit being so sorry for everything?" Her silverware rattled in her setup with the force of her hand coming down on the table.

"What do you want from me? Just tell me what to do and I'll do it."

Our waitress arrived with the food. Angela unfurled her napkin and carefully placed each piece of silverware exactly where she wanted it. I had to be careful to not eat too quickly. I hadn't had an appetite in months. That night I felt like devouring entire farms.

"How's your steak? That is, if you can taste the meat under all that crispiness."

I had to finish crunching before I could speak. "It's good, thanks. How's yours?"

"Can't complain."

"Always the optimist."

"It's good. Sorry."

"No. It's okay."

We cut and chewed.

"What do you expect from tonight?"

"You called me."

"I'm aware of that."

"What would have happened if you'd come over last night

like you'd wanted?"

"I never said I wanted to come over."

I tried to keep my face emotionless. Chew, chew, chew.

"I did want to come over. It's so hard to come home—home. God, I hate using that word for that place. I feel the desire to leave as soon as I set foot in there. My bed was empty. It was late. I gave in. I was weak and I called you."

"What would have happened if I was weak and told you to come over?"

"What are you trying to prove?"

I put a piece of steak in my mouth, silent.

"We would've ended up fighting or fucking and we'd be in no different a place today as yesterday, I suppose."

"I want nothing more than to help you feel better. Anything I can do, let me know. I'll do anything."

"If I knew, I'd ask. I don't know that you're what can help me now."

"I'm the source. Confronting your pain always makes it easier. At least a bit."

"This isn't easy for me."

"It's not exactly easy for me either." I put my fork down. "I mean, I know it's harder for you, though." We both had to confront my capacity for evil.

"You got any ideas about how to make this all stop? What should I do? Tell me."

"I don't know. If I did I would."

"I'm going to regret saying this," she twirled her fork in the air like she would if she were eating spaghetti, "but I kinda wish we could get away for a night or two and be alone together. Go somewhere neutral and just try to figure out what to do. Maybe reconnect a bit, you know? I don't know. What do you think?"

"You would want to do that?"

"If you said let's go now, I'd say okay."

My heart was racing fast enough to power two bodies. "Really?"

She nodded once. She looked pained as she did this, as though she was being forced to say this.

"Yeah. Let's do it. I'd love to. I'll get the check. You drive." She always said I was a terrible driver.

The key card wouldn't work. I secretly believed she just didn't have the touch, that if I were operating it, the door would crumble simply because I willed it. "There'd better be a mini-fridge," she said as she finally turned the light green.

"I don't think I've ever stayed in a hotel room with a mini-fridge before."

"Are you serious?"

"Always. Totally." We hadn't said much on the drive, but being near each other in that confined space had settled us. We were getting closer to being ourselves again.

I threw my jacket on a waiting-room chair with print like a preloaded computer desktop background and took in my surroundings. Furniture made of a material equal distance between wood and plastic, bed with matching desktop-print comforter, delivery menus, sink, bathroom and, by god, a mini-fridge. It was the nicest hotel room I'd ever been in. Angela had an elevating effect on me.

"Anything good in there?" I asked.

"The usual. M&Ms, some booze. Nothing too great."

"Think if I break this seal they'll charge me for it?"

"Probably."

"Oh well." I cracked open the welcome kit and dumped the contents onto the bed. "Shampoo, soap, lots of gum. Three razors for you and three for me. There are more razors in here than packets of shampoo."

"There's no shaving gel either."

"This place is so elegant, but still has so many flaws."

"It suits us."

"I guess so."

"I wish we had a black light." She grinned at the bed like she'd already scoured it for stains.

"I certainly do not."

"Come on. It'd be fun."

"The less I know, the more comfortable I'll be."

I was relieved that she was the first to plop down.

"This is almost fun, huh?" It was fun, but I wasn't willing to chance putting my emotion on her.

"I'm enjoying myself. God, I haven't said that in forever."

"I know. Me too."

"So now what?"

"I don't know. Do we just pretend? Try to act like everything's okay? Like this is our bunker at the end of the world?"

"If this is our bunker we're gonna need more supplies," she held a cold domestic beer that shined in the hotel lighting. "Wait. Is this okay? Would you prefer I didn't?"

"No. Go ahead. Be yourself."

"Are you sure?"

"It's fine."

She put the beer back and closed the fridge door.

From the bathroom she said, "Why didn't we ever shower together?"

"I don't know. You never asked."

"You could've asked, too."

"If you would've asked I would've done it."

"Maybe later."

I wanted to jump all over this, cling to it like a husband clings to his wife's wedding ring, discovered miraculously still intact in the burnt wreckage, but I let it sit and linger in the recycled hotel air until it was taken up by the vent and thrown down into the background of some other room, of someone else's story.

Suddenly she turned toward me. "Why didn't you ever take responsibility for what you did?"

"What?"

"You've never told me that it was all your fault."

I knew I had. I had to. Those late-night phone conversations where roles were reversed and she was the drunk one. "It was all my fault."

"It doesn't make a difference at this point."

"Probably not much does."

"You're right," she said.

"If there is any chance of there ever being an 'us' again, I am absolutely committed to fighting for it. I would do anything to make that happen. I love you so much."

"It feels good to know that."

"Does that mean there's a chance, then?"

"I'd like to think so. I wish. But probably not."

"If we both want it, we can make it happen."

"I can't change who you are."

"I'm not asking you to. I can change me, though. I have. I'm different now. I mean, I'm the same too. Some things you can't change." I took her hand. "It'll never happen again."

She took her hand back.

"I know you can't believe that. But I know it to my innermost core. It'll never happen again."

"It'd be nice to be able to believe that. But I can't trust you. At all. I want to, but I can't."

This crushed me, like finding out your marriage is nullified. One of my innermost foundations had been shaken—no, not just shaken, but toppled. "It takes time to trust in the first place. I'd imagine, and maybe I'm wrong, tell me if I am, I don't want to interpret your feelings through myself, it'd take longer to trust me after I've broken your trust. Done that to you. What I'm saying is, with enough time and accountability, that trust could be repaired." That was what the recovery book said.

"I can't put myself in that situation. I can't let you hurt me again."

"I won't."

"Here we are again."

"Yeah."

We stared into each other's eyes without ever actually making eye contact.

"Look," I said, trying not to furrow my brow too deeply, "as much as I'd love to get you back, it matters more to me that you're okay. That you're able to heal. Doing that to you was the most terrible thing I've ever done. Her. I've never hurt anyone like that before. I've done my share of stupid things, but it's always been at my own expense. Hurting you like that is the only regret I have."

"I'm glad I get to be your first."

"I don't want you to be. I want to fix this."

"If I knew what to do, I would."

"I know. Maybe we'll figure it out here."

"Maybe."

"I wish we had a deck of cards or something to do that wasn't sit here with all this weight on us."

She reached into her purse. "It's a habit I picked up. You have a bottle opener on your keychain, I carry a deck of cards. You'd be surprised how often it comes in handy."

"You are an amazing woman."

She smiled and shuffled.

"Have I ever won a game against you?"

"I don't think so."

"How is that possible? It's all luck."

"You know what they say, 'Unlucky at cards, lucky at love.'"

"Let's keep playing then. A couple more games and you'll be falling all over me."

"We'll see about that."

I couldn't sleep. I lay awake trying to think of ways to prolong our stay. The desk clerk never asked how many beds we needed. I had interpreted this as a good sign. It meant we looked like we belonged in the same bed. When the time came, I still offered to sleep on the floor. "Don't be silly," she said as she pulled off her dress. I laid as far away from her unclothed body as the bed would allow. I couldn't do it, couldn't lay there with her warmth aching next to me. I wrapped an arm around her and she didn't pull away. Nothing was wrong. Everything was exactly as it should be. I couldn't let go of her, of this. I needed to make this last forever. We were safe there. If I fell asleep, there was no way to guarantee she'd be there in the morning. I wished I knew what to say to make her stay.

"Let's get room service."

Neither of us was used to this sort of decadence, but it felt right. We ordered enough food to last until checkout time: a large pizza, spaghetti with meatballs, French fries, two pieces of cheesecake and a couple beers for her. The meatballs were mushy, like undercooked soy meat.

The pizza was gone. "I only ate two pieces," she said.

"I know. Sorry. I was hungry I guess."

"I guess so."

"I have a control problem, okay."

"Trust me, I know," she said as she gulped off her beer bottle. They had brought up actual glass bottles.

"The worst of it is over. Not a sip. Not a drop. Nothing. Any time I think about it, I picture the look of agony on your face I have pasted into my memory. That's one of the few things I actually remember from that night."

"Stop using that crutch."

"I know you don't want to hear it, but it's a big part of it. I do have a control problem. And it only gets worse once I start to indulge myself. How much did I say to you while eating that pizza?"

"I don't know. I was eating."

"I get so self-absorbed. I'd like to think I'm a selfless person, but sometimes I let go and there's nothing in the world besides what's in front of me. I can control this, at least to a point, but there are certain times, certain things that block that for me. If I'd never had any of that pizza I would have never finished it, and if I hadn't been blind drunk I would have never done whatever I did with her."

"Stop."

"Sure, the temptation would have been there, but I could have controlled it. I'm not blaming the drinking. I know you think I am, but I'm not. My drinking is a part of me, a personality defect. I'm blaming myself. I'm taking full responsibility for my actions. I'm taking action to make sure it'll never happen again. Drinking wasn't necessarily the root, but it was the catalyst, and without a match, dynamite will never explode."

"We've been through this already."

"I know, but I don't think you understand what I'm getting at."

"No, I get it. It still isn't a guarantee. I can never allow you to hurt me like that again. I won't do it."

"There's no way I could bear to hurt you like that again. I don't know how I made it through this time. I never realized how much power to hurt you I had."

"I wish I could forgive you and move on and be with you. I've tried. I can't, though. You cheated on me."

"I don't remember doing it. I know it's true, but I don't remember."

"I can't get past this. I want to, but I don't think I can."

"If we work on it together, we can. We're good at this. Our relationship was full of problems. We'd always iron them out. We can do this. If we both want it then it can happen. I'm willing to be here for you for as long as it takes."

"Thanks."

"I'll do anything for you. As long as it takes, I'll be waiting. You're worth it."

"I don't see how you couldn't have known how much you'd hurt me."

I looked at her, on the verge of tears, and broke down crying. "I love you so much. I don't want this to be the last time I tell you."

She pulled me into her arms and held me against her breasts as I cried. I kept repeating that I was sorry, that it shouldn't be like this, I never wanted to hurt her. I felt awful, but her grip comforted me, made me feel safe. "Tell me what I should do. Tell me how to fix this, how to help you."

"I don't know. Whatever it is has to help us."

"Us separately or together?" I stopped sniveling for a second and looked into her eyes set into that face like a thousand porcelain dolls. She pulled me to her mouth and kissed me. That kiss like hope, like being on the brim of the future, like a kept promise, let me know I was still alive.

"I almost wanted to call that making love."

"Seems fitting to me." She merged onto the freeway.

"Now what?"

"I don't know."

"Can I call you?"

"Let me move at my own pace."

"Sure. I understand."

"That is, if I have a pace at all."

"Of course. Absolutely. I understand." I knew at that time, in the depths of my heart that she would forgive me, that we would be together forever and that someday we'd be old and happy together. I felt there was no other way for us to end.

Graeagle

Before her keys even hit the dish, he's talking. "We should go up to the mountains, spend the weekend in Graeagle."

"Tonight? Now?" she asks, weary at the thought of a four-hour drive at night through the wilderness.

"Now. You said we've lost spontaneity. Let's go."

"We'll check in so late. Is it even worth it?"

"It's always worth it. You say that every time. It's gorgeous right now. Let's go."

She thinks about her day at work. How six hours makes her feel like eight used to and ten before that. Her knees. Even with the chair they gave her, her knees still ache. The pain reminds her of the sound of a food mill.

The car. She'd have to drive. His eyesight is waning and he won't admit it, won't admit anything. To drive at night, he throws a hand over his left eye just to get part of a clear picture.

"Why?" she asks.

"I promise you'll never forget this trip. It'll be the trip to end all trips."

Normally he doesn't speak in these grandiose terms. His face is crimson with flashes of white, like salami. There's an omnipotent glow emanating from him. He has a plan. Not since he asked her to marry him has he looked like this.

Actually, he asked her to marry him up there. The heat of high-altitude summer. The crisp blue glass of Frenchman Lake. Quiet enough that the two of them may have been the only people left in the world. "Yes," even though she'd given the matter no thought before. Graeagle has that sort of effect on people.

She says yes, and after a confidently uneventful drive, they arrive at River Pines, without a reservation and late. Someone always stays on the premises, and tonight it's Max, wily old Frenchman and stiff drink pourer, that they awaken. He remembers them. Somehow he remembers all the regulars despite the year lapse in their presence. "This is not your time," he says. He rubs the sleep out of his eyes but leaves the wildfire of his hair untamed.

"It's a special occasion," her husband says.

"Do you have anything available?" she says, knowing Max would give them his own bed if he had to.

"Not your regular cabin. Not a cabin at all. A hotel unit. Not so much romantic. A cabin is open for tomorrow if you wish to move."

"The hotel unit is fine," her husband says. "Through Sunday, please."

"But of course. The register is shut down. Pay tomorrow. Number one three two. Do you wish for help with your bags?"

"We only brought one each. Thanks, though," she says as she grabs the key.

They've never seen a hotel unit here, but it's the same as anywhere. She wonders what sort of magic can happen here, can happen anywhere.

He fills a plastic cup with water and says, "I know this is the same water we have at home, but it simply tastes better up here." In one long pull he finishes his cup and pours another. "I want to sit outside and see the stars. I miss them. Care to join me?"

Tired and ready to relax her way into sleep, she says yes. They sit side by side on the most comfortable hard plastic picnic table in the world. Slowly, he sips at his water. He is quiet, reverent even.

She cannot sit any longer. Her body, her brain. When she tells him she's going to bed he says, "I'll be in before it's too late." She lays in bed alone. Through the doorway they left open so the room could breathe he says, "I hope you know I will always love you."

"I know that," she says. "Goodnight."

Without him next to her, she cannot sleep. Perhaps she dozes off briefly a couple times, but she does not really sleep. He comes inside later than she'd expected. She hears him remove his clothes. She feels the chill of his body before he even touches her. His body is ice cold against hers in bed. He won't warm up.

"Do you want me to turn the heater on?" she asks, even though she's hot, wrapped up in the blankets.

He doesn't respond. There is no city nearby, so there is no light pollution to help her find the heater in the dark; she turns on the lamp beside the bed. He does not stir. Normally so sensitive to light, and he does not stir.

Gently she asks, "Are you alright?" and sits next to him.

She sees now his eyes are open.

Knowing just what he would have wanted, she turns the light off and crawls back into bed. She will call the coroner in the morning.

Acid Trip

We were laying in bed watching TV, recuperating from the previous night, when she said, "Want to drop acid?"

I replied, "I've never done it before."

"Me neither. But it's only one tab. I don't think anything will happen." And just like that my fear was nullified—all the thoughts of jumping off buildings, forgetting reality, the scare stories, all of it disappeared.

I said, "Sure. What do we do?"

"I'll cut it in two. I think you just let it soak into your tongue." She placed the little paper on the center of my sense of taste and said, "Cheers."

I was fully prepared for space travel, for magic. We soaked LSD down into our spines and waited.

Was TV especially funny tonight? I felt laughter emanating from my belly like smoke out of a soon-to-erupt volcano. "Do you feel anything funny going on?" I struggled to get out.

"No. Nothing," she said, serious as a crime show.

Maybe I was making it up; false anticipation, like tricking yourself you are in love after knowing someone for three weeks. No. I definitely felt something. All true personal evaluations occur in the bathroom. I looked into the mirror and started to question my own reality; my mind suddenly broke down and realigned itself post-structurally. There was a painting of a ghostly girl holding a Siamese cat on the wall; the cat's pupils were contracting and expanding like black holes.

"I am decidedly tripping," I muttered as I came out of the bathroom. Light trails started, draining my vision like a lifetime drains the soul. She laughed. And laughed and laughed and laughed. "I need to be naked."

She followed my lead and stripped like she was my reflecting pool. I lay down on the bed next to her body, skin touching like seven hundred sensitive silkworms slithering slanted or my surface melting point or puddles of rainbows dripping down the wall.

It was amazing.

We touched for hours. Or clock hands going around clockwise several times on the melting clocks I saw. And then, finally, my brain cleared up a bit and I said to myself or out loud, "If this is this, then imagine a kiss." I kissed her neck. I sucked. I bit. I loved. Sounds came from her or the bed of goose feathers beneath her flesh like pleasure or pain or experience or false, but I'd started and I wasn't stopping until this was over.

Then I remembered sex. Penis in vagina. There. There it is. Yes. Dragons blowing fire to start up a sunrise. Sensual massage in a hot shower. Happy Endings. Our bodies were molding. Molting pieces of each, all the unnecessaries, the extraneous, to become one. We were the same. I. Her. Me. You. Meaningless.

There was so much meaning going on.

I got off like the secrets of the universe revealed. Cross-eyed, falling off. Death. Transcend.

"Wow," both of us speaking in unison. We started pulling apart like taffy. Slowly. Coming down. Slower. Almost regular.

Back in the bathroom. More self-realization? No. The black holes were there, but moving slower, further out in space. There was still some chemical effect on my body, but it was different, tweakier, more mechanical, gears and short-circuited wires. I started twitching. A fogginess beneath my skin. I was about to start grinding my teeth. Strung out. She was asleep in bed. I lay down next to her, spooned and hoped for the best. Once my hand found its nook below her ribs I calmed down. Asleep before the side effects took over.

Cokedumpster

She rolls over so she's no longer facing the TV. This means she's going to sleep. This means I'm not getting laid.

She called a couple hours ago. No, five hours. Shit. Where'd the time go? She called and said, "Yeah, sure. We can hang out." I was already sleeping when she called. Last night was still strong in my body. "What did that last part of your message say?"

"Huh? Oh yeah." I pulled my balls off my leg. "I said, 'This shit ain't gonna snort itself.'"

"Yeah, let's definitely hang out."

I only had leftovers from last night, so I expected to get a little high, fuck and then pass out. She was carrying, too. Of course we did it all. I was fucking high. Too fucking high. Too fucking high to fuck. About the time I start to come down, about the time I'm ready to fuck, is when she rolls over. I think about just going for it anyway. I know she came over here planning on fucking. I know she wants it. She's snoring. Now if I go for it, it's rape. Great. Maybe I could jerk it. My mattress is designed to transfer as little motion to my sleepmate as possible. Very expensive. But if she wakes up, I'm a pervert. I resign myself to going to bed horny. What I'll do is, when I wake up I'll give her sweet little kisses all over her body. Not a broad in the world can resist wake-up kisses. I'll be fucking her before she's even awake enough to know what's happening.

I have to piss. Now. I know this before I'm even awake. Now. Piss. Go. My dick is hard. I piss all over.

I'm still hard when I get back to my bedroom. She's here. I forgot. My dick is throbbing. I lay down next to her. I'm wide awake. I don't feel like I slept that long. Did I dream about fucking her? I'm definitely still horny as fuck. What time is it? My phone's on the other side of her so I get up to look at it. It's already noon.

Fuck it. I'm going to fuck her. I wish this erection would go down for a minute. It can't be the first thing she feels when she wakes up. I'm kissing her, careful to keep my dick back. She stirs. "Mmm. What time is it?"

"I don't know," between mouthfuls of meat.

She grabs my phone off the end table. "Fuck. It's late." I keep kissing her. It's time. I press my pelvis up against her ass. "What are you doing?"

"Waking you up." Thrust.

"Hey, stop it. I'm up." I keep going. "Get off me."

"What?"

"No. Not when I first wake up."

I flop off her onto my side of the bed. My hands are locked behind my head. My dick is waving like a flag.

"Look. Where is this going?"

"I was trying to fuck you."

"I know. I mean, like, what's the point? We've been doing this for a few months. I come over. We do some drugs. Fuck. Sleep. It's fun, but what's the point?"

"I'm enjoying myself."

"Don't get me wrong, me too."

"So what's the problem?" Finally, my dick goes soft.

"I just don't get it. I think I need some time to myself to figure some things out. I'm sure you understand."

"Yeah, totally."

"We can still be friends."

"Sure."

Why the fuck was she here so long? What possesses someone to stay in the bed of the guy she just rejected? What a sick fuck. I'm upset. I am. I wasn't that attached to her, but I was starting to get attached. Maybe. Some. Enough that I'm upset. At least a little. I wish I had saved some coke. I'm still horny. How can I be upset if I'm still horny?

Horny overrides upset. I turn my computer on. The bitch on the screenshot of Throated! looks just like her. It's uncanny.

The first girl's mascara is running all over. She's been crying. She looks drugged.

The next slut is emaciated. The guy rips her hair back as he fucks the back of her throat. With the amount of makeup covering this cumdumpster's face I know there's something nasty beneath. She's frothing at the mouth.

I finally click on the whore that looks like her. She whimpers. She says, "Let me suck that for you."

She retches. "Oh God, I love that," she says. She's choking, gasping for breath. The cock gags her. She can't fucking breathe. It's like watching a murder. Semen shoots from my penis. Tears shoot from my eyes.

Worth It

The yellow UPS Post-It Note stuck to my building's front door yesterday said the package would arrive by 4:00 and it was now 6:30. I'd waited all day and the buzzer hadn't rung. I was starving, which meant I had to leave my apartment because I was out of food. I don't seem to ever have food around. I don't understand.

I went downstairs and looked in my mailbox; there was guaranteed to be no brown UPS box, but maybe a new magazine would come, a consolation prize.

And there it was on the heavy glass front door: a new Post-It Note from UPS. Final Delivery. Must come in if you wish to receive your package. You have one week or it will be returned to sender. To Sensationalities, Inc.

Fucking hell damn shit. Did they even try to ring my buzzer? Assholes.

I was planning to just go to the corner store to pick up eggs because they were the first thing inside the door and I could grab them and get home faster than a heart attack, but there was no longer a need to rush, so I took all the time I deserved and went to New Ganges for lamb curry and woodstove naan. I even got mango lassi afterward.

I went home and tried to find a bus that would go to the industrial area where UPS was located. Nothing. Riding the bus with a package that big would be a pain in the ass anyways. I would have to pay for a cab to the nowhereness of industrial areas. Warehouses just aren't built where they are useful.

It wouldn't be a cheap journey, and I had spent almost my

whole bank account on materializing the package in the first place. I would have to cut back somewhere. No more New Ganges; just eggs, beans, rice. Ketchup would now be a vegetable and water would be milk.

I called Checkered Cab and ordered a ride at 9:00 the next morning.

All night I was excited as a virgin going to prom. I knew the package would change my life. If it weren't for masturbation, I would have never calmed down enough to sleep that night.

The next morning I showered, blow dried and flat ironed my hair, put on mascara, slipped on my blue polka dot dress and went outside at 8:50. I skipped breakfast.

The cab came at 9:03 and I watched the meter rise all the way to Hegenberger and Pardee.

"Could you give me a hand carrying this?"

"The meter stays on."

"I know." Fucking greedy bitch. I fucking know.

It didn't fit in the trunk; it was too wide, so we folded down the passenger seat and laid it there. I sat behind the driver.

Even though we were turned around to go back home, the meter kept going in the same direction.

"How about a hand getting this upstairs?" I tried to flirt, but I didn't know how exactly. Which is why I needed my package at all. I just softened my voice.

"Meter keeps running."

I blinked twice to cover my eye roll. "Okay."

I wanted to go straight into my apartment, rip open my box and never leave again. I went downstairs with the driver to complete the transaction.

"How much do I owe you, big boy?" Ugh. I sounded like a fledgling '50s sexual object.

"Fifty-seven twenty-five," he said, oblivious to my ogling.

I handed him my money and just fucking went for it. I kissed him so I wouldn't have to tip him.

He blinked, then tried to look like this happens all the time. I would have to go further.

He gave me my change and waited, expecting to get it all back. I gave it to him, but in a foreign currency. I kissed him again, this time with more tongue. I grabbed his hands and put one on my breast and one on my ass for good measure. "Thanks."

"No. Thank you miss. You know, things can be done to refund your money to you, you know."

I welcomed the opportunity to prostitute myself with open

arms, like the old, sagging whore who finally turns a trick after being on the corner every night for a week. "Come on up."

It was totally fucking pleasureless, physically speaking, but mentally I was exuberant at saving sixty bucks. I didn't take off my dress. At least he was quick. And left after he smoked a cigarette. He gave me back my money, put on his pants and walked out the door without speaking.

I jumped up like his penis had when he realized he might get laid and opened my package. There was the Pleasurenator 2000, my new Fucking Machine, fully assembled. I jumped on and pedaled myself to orgasm faster than the spread of AIDS in the '80s.

I fucked myself all day long, only stopping long enough to breathe.

For lunch I put it up my butt. For dinner I used the auto-drive.

Tonight, I couldn't sleep because of masturbation. I ended up fucking myself senseless and passed out at sunrise, still with the plastic dick inside me.

I woke up around noon and started pedaling my way through a new day.

I came twelve times in three hours. The thirteenth time was taking longer, I could tell, even through my pleasure parade. Then my heart started beating faster, irregularly, like jumbling dice in a cup. My neck twitched and I screamed, "My god. This is the big one. What I've always waited for!" Then it was my arms, rubbing my nipples in spasmodic glee, jerking, twitching, jumping, maybe even convulsing. And I swear I felt my heart stop, but didn't care because I knew this was the greatest feeling of all time, like a million hands rubbing your body from the inside and each set is trained in a different art of massage. And I felt the hands stop my pulse. And one set closed up my lungs. And one hand whomped my vocal cords with a karate chop to produce a gurgling *urgh* like a last gasp for breath or a first moan of orgasm.

And I fucked myself to death.

And it was so fucking worth it.

Welcome To The Neighborhood

first published online by Barrier Islands Review

I've been watching. They've been hammering, painting, drilling, reconstructing, changing. I'm watching the foreman in his oxford shirt—a symbol of his future—and hardhat—a nod to his past—walk around with a clipboard, checking things off his list. Since this little project got started, the foreman's been there every day but the day Teraq came over to play cards and the day Bodie got hauled in. He talks more than anything. Everyone else grunts their way through the day; he finesses. Once in a while he'll pick up a hammer in a huff and berate his workers with each swing. He's the only one there now, putting on the finishing touches. I haven't seen a full crew around in a week. Since the first, when the suburbs moved in.

I introduced myself. I saw the moving truck so big you'd need a special license to drive the thing and hobbled out to my stoop. I am the welcoming committee and sentinel of the community. It's my job; no, my duty to check out the immigrants and scope out their intentions. I wanted to give them the benefit of the doubt. Don't judge a book—even one written by the devil himself—by its cover. I was ready to offer my services. I spent a few months as a mover back in the day. I could've given superb lifting advice. That gigantic, bulky TV looked near impossible to lift for those three scrawny kids. Probably the first piece of real work those softhands ever did.

"Welcome to the neighborhood. I'm Vince." I smiled at the pretty little girl with the big ass first.

"Thanks. I'm Annah. This is Allison." Her hair was almost

translucent and cut a couple knuckles short. The girls stepped closer, into the street. The third one, the male, stood back, sizing me up. They looked like the clothing ads on the backs of magazines.

"I'm Adam," he looked back and jerked his head in mild acknowledgment. He continued to strain up the stairs with box in tow.

"What brings you girls to the neighborhood?"

"Our apartment wasn't really big enough. We got a dog and need the yard space."

"We're really excited to move to the area. There's so much potential." They wrapped arms around each other. There was nothing I could do. I waved and went back inside. I kept watching.

The next time I saw any of them outside the house—I saw them inside enough to know mommy and daddy were paying the bills—I was waiting on the stoop for BeBe to come back from the corner store with my chips. The white guy was unloading Whole Foods bags from his bright green Honda, newer than most models in the neighborhood. He had to know I was watching, but he never looked up, never waved. He chose to remain blissfully ignorant of his surroundings, secluded like a subdivision.

I've been aware of everything—every game of dice, every funeral, every feast—in this neighborhood for over fifty years. I was born in this house. I planned on dying here. I've seen what this community was. I see what it is. I fear for where it's headed. We're headed out. They're coming in. These ones across the street are far from the first. Before, we had the artists and the punks—mostly harmless, a bit destructive and outsiderly, which kept property values stagnant, but white and safe nonetheless. These three are the first of a new breed, though. Suburban youth. The entitled class looking for the chic guiltlessness of poverty. We're the last neighborhood left standing in this city. It's an epidemic of economics. For the longest time we all thought we were immune to it. None of us have much longer.

When the developer bought the house across the street, I talked to him about his plans. It's my job to do things like this. No one else was rushing out to talk to the blue-shirt, red-tie, white-face businessman.

"This neighborhood's changing," he said. "It's on its way up. I can feel it. I'm getting in on the ground floor. I'm fixing this place up. The profit potential is phenomenal. Nowhere to go but up." He hasn't been back since. He hired contractors who hired aliens to come in and do the grunt work. There are so many families without jobs in the neighborhood. I watched as they rebuilt that house from the inside out like an infection. Now those kids live in the nicest house in the neighborhood. Everywhere else there are shiftless cars on blocks and unpainted walls, half-open chain link fences and broken glass.

The developer has been exercising his connections downtown to put pressure on the corner store. He wants them out. Too many kids hanging around in front, must be up to no good. The same family has owned the store since before I was born. I've never seen any real trouble there. They keep their business safe. The only cars that creep through this neighborhood where there are bars on street-facing windows are Beamers now. They're prospecting around here more and more often. We are the nearby lake the mining company pollutes without conscience.

They're ruining our neighborhood. We worked so hard to get it here and now they're going to take it away. Used to be worse, much worse. Someone on near every corner slanging. But then we went through the process, the community outreach, counseling, helped ourselves and got it pretty clean. The drugs are still here, always will be, just like they'll always be on Wall Street too, but we got rid of the violence. No more bullets crossing jump rope lines. Suppose that's what drew these kids here. That's our market potential.

I feel like I'm the only one who notices this stuff. I'm the only one to ever bring it up. When people stop by my stoop, they all try to remain optimistic and good-humored, look at the bright side, it won't happen to us. They think they have rights. They think because they've been here forever they're okay. I shove the cold truth right into their faces. We're lying to ourselves. It's a fact. They want us out of here. Market potential, something we'll never be a part of, is too strong and uncaring a force for us to reckon with. They will get their land, they always have, they always will. No one knows how to stop them. Millions have tried and millions have died. The market is too big for us. This is not as it should be. We live here. We should have full autonomy over what happens to us. I am fuming, pacing on my stoop like a stark-raving lunatic of an old man. Something has to be done. The powers that be won't do it for us. I have to take this matter into my own hands.

BeBe stops by on his way to the store to see if I need anything. I'm on my stoop for this sole hopeful purpose.

"I don't. No." I answer as a formality. Don't look too anxious. These things must be done coolly. I've been here long enough to know that.

"You alright, Pops?"

"No one's home," I nod toward the house across the street.

"They got a dog."

"In the backyard."

"No shit?" These kids are clearly mock-slumming it, living out their ghetto fantasies. People from here don't make that sort of mistake.

BeBe lives two houses down, born and probably die too. He's a good kid. A bit unsavory maybe, but a good kid. I'm his wisdom of the world. At least I tried to be. Sometimes this world is too much for one man. The world got to BeBe and there is nothing I can do to change that. He is what he is. The world is what it is. I cannot change that, only influence it in the direction I want it to go.

Time passes as I sit and watch the house. I watch two kids sit on the stoop. Three more lounge on their feet behind. I can't see him, but I imagine BeBe's behind them, prying open the door. They're subtle. They're practiced. I know what's going on and I can't see. Someone always has a cigarette in his hand. They're just kids, hanging out on a stoop, got no place else to go, wanna do good, just ain't no jobs, nothing productive to do so we sit and watch.

I can see the door is open now. I don't see anyone go in. They're still just hanging out. BeBe's the only one inside. This is beautiful. This is the reclamation of my life.

BeBe practically hurdles the sitting-down kids. They all scatter off like there are red and blue lights flashing nearby. Something isn't right. They shouldn't look so panicked. It was supposed to be easy. He wasn't in there long enough. Something isn't right.

I'm pounding on BeBe's security screen door. "BeBe! BeBe!" I'm yelling. No one's coming. I don't give up. I won't give up. This has to work. I have to save us.

"What you doing off your stoop Pops?" It comes from behind me.

"What happened? I handed that house to you."

"You handed me a shithole. Missing walls. There's still bullet holes in the window from when that crackhead shot it out. And they ain't got shit but weird-ass little knickknacks and shit. Like gnomes and toys and shit. I managed to get one measly fucking old ass laptop before the alarm went off."

I don't say anything. I don't move. Alarm, I think. These kids truly are of a new breed. As BeBe walks into his house he turns back and says, "Go! Fuck up outta here old man!" The screen rattles shut. BeBe's gone. He thinks I'm senile, can't even tell who's worth robbing. He wants me out of his life. He doesn't realize he wouldn't be here without me. Without me fighting to keep this neighborhood for us he couldn't be here. He doesn't think about these things. He'll hang out at home and get a chance to relax and I'll go back to my window and watch. I'll keep this neighborhood safe for us.

I watch to see what is going on around here. I see nothing. Anytime the cops show up, the block dies. No matter why they're here, they kill us every time.

But the neighborhood persists. Kids start throwing balls to and fro in the street again, the yelling din of domestic disputes makes itself known and the liquor store becomes its own sovereign state. Everything feels normal. I haven't seen anyone from the house across the street since they were openly cooperating with the cops when I went to bed the other night.

Someone knocks on my door. Since things have calmed down and returned to normal, I've been able to relax a bit, to take a much needed and deserved vacation. I'm watching TV, so I didn't see them come up the stairs. I peek through the missing slats of the blinds to see the white guy from across the street. Everyone, even the most recent, least-welcome immigrants, knows I'm always here. I can't just hope he leaves like I want to. I have to go to the door. I have to face my murderer.

My hands tug up and in to the click then down and in to get the door open. The security screen door will stay in place. I stick my head out and leave my body behind the frame.

"Hey. Vince, is it?" He's not making eye contact. I have him intimidated. I keep staring. Talking will only reveal myself. "I don't know if you noticed at all, but the other night my house got robbed. It's the one across the street." His fingers are wiping against his palms. His eyes shift along the door frame. "We just moved in last week. I'm pretty sure we met." He pauses to receive confirmation. I give him less acknowledgment than he's ever given me. "Right. And I guess the frame of the door wasn't put into the house right and it's sorta the landlord's fault and not that much was taken and at least we're all safe and okay. A bit shaken, but all right really. The whole thing's a huge mess and well, my computer was taken and there was a ton of really important stuff on there. I work for a non-profit that's meant to help educate and provide long-term employment to the lower class. Good jobs too, room for advancement. We're starting a green-collar program which should be huge in the future. It's really exciting. I'm super excited, but we're in trouble without that computer. I don't know what I'll do without all that info. It's all gone. The whole non-profit's in jeopardy and I just need it back. I'm really stressing about this. I feel like I'm about to lose my mind. What I'm trying to get at is, did you see anything? It'd mean so much to me."

He's trying to help. His efforts are wildly misguided—we can save ourselves, don't need some rich white guy coming into our neighborhood to save us. I can save us. "As a matter of fact, this college kid-looking guy just came and tried to sell me a computer." I want this kid off my stoop and this tale is the quickest way to get him out of here. He wouldn't understand the truth, doesn't know the reality of this neighborhood, didn't grow up here. He'd tell me I was wrong.

His face lights up with hope I know to be false. "College kid like how?" The laptop is gone for good. If this kid belonged here he would know that, know nothing—no one—ever comes back here.

"You know, beard and longer hair, brown. About your height too. White." He should know there's no white kid going around stealing things in this neighborhood.

"Did you see the computer?"

"No. I knew it had to be stolen so I got him out of here fast as I could."

"About how long ago?"

"Maybe half an hour."

"Thank you so much. You've been such a help. Let me know if there's ever anything I can do for you. Please."

"Hey, you ain't gonna send the cops over here are you?"

"No. If it'd been up to me, the cops would've never been involved in this. The alarm that the piece-of-shit landlord insisted be put in, I totally don't want it there, went off and called in the cops. Not much I could do. I filed a report just in case the landlord has insurance that will cover it or can be put at fault for the shoddy door, but that's about it. No one trusts a cop. I mean, no one saw anything so the report won't hurt. It's not like the cops are going to try to hunt someone down for stealing a laptop from a non-profit nobody. Maybe if I was an oil tycoon I'd stand a chance. Whatever. Hey, thank you so much for your help. Again, if I can ever help you out just let me know. I should really get going so I can see if there's any chance of hunting this guy down. I mean, I know there's not, but it's worth a shot. Everyone needs hope."

Of course there's no way he'll find the guy. Even if the guy did exist, he wouldn't track him down. This neighborhood is a vacuum.

Riverwest

Three of us had signed the lease for April 15, but we would illegally house a fourth—in Milwaukee only three unrelated humans could rent one domicile. Supposedly the law started out as three unrelated women, to prevent brothels from forming, and somewhere along the way it came to include men. There were two bedrooms upstairs, along with a full bath. On the main level was the living room, dining room, kitchen, another bedroom and a half bath. I would live in the basement.

The house was in the heart of Riverwest, on Center Street, across from what was then Onopa, a club for smaller touring bands. Soon enough, Riverwest would become the hip neighborhood for young white kids to live in, but not yet. It was downtrodden and nonwhite. Dangerous, but we were invincible. Milwaukee was not racially integrated anywhere, but Riverwest was the closest the city came. It was possible to see a black guy and a Puerto Rican woman on the same block, something impossible elsewhere in Milwaukee. We weren't trying to bust down socioeconomic barriers when we signed the lease; for us, it was cheap.

Like the rest of Riverwest, the house had been a wasteland before, but it was changing. It had been a crack house. The rental company bought the property cheap and put in new walls, floors, appliances and windows. The house was still under construction when we viewed it, but the contractor scoffed at the notion of not being finished in time.

The work wasn't done on time. My friends' leases extended into May. I only had until April 15. I begged and pleaded with the rental company. Eventually they relented and let me put my things in the basement until the work was done. I was allowed to put my bed upstairs. I couldn't set up my illegal bedroom in the basement out of fear that our four-person home would be discovered.

The work was supposed to be done in three days; it was not. Then in two more days; it was not. Then in three more days; it was not. I came home Saturday to a house that looked the same as it had on Monday. "Jesus Christ!" My voice echoed in the expansive emptiness, calling out to no one. The closet doors were lying next to their hinges. There were no towel racks nor vent covers. There were no door stops nor blinds. The mailbox was on the kitchen counter. I tried to be thankful I had somewhere to sleep. I wasn't, though. I expected the work to be done.

I was nowhere. Not at home, not homeless. I was going crazy from only getting five hours of sleep a night, as I was woken each morning by the grinding of saws. The hollowness of a new home. That space was so empty. It wasn't like when your roommates go on vacation and there's furniture and televisions to keep you company and keep the house quiet. It wasn't like a one-bedroom apartment where the space is designed for single occupancy. That behemoth of a house engulfed me. I was utterly alone in the world. I felt like I was drifting through space, existing in a vacuum. All I wanted was to live.

New houses click. I expected it to creak—that's what happens in campfire stories—so I wouldn't have been surprised to hear wood expand and contract and moan orgasmically, but click? I didn't know what to do about that. I wasn't supposed to bring anything upstairs to keep me company and cover the house's wails, but, since the workers' days ended at noon on weekdays, I figured no one would show up on a Saturday, so I brought my TV and DVD player into my temporary room. I poured myself a powerful mix of whiskey and soda and put in a movie. I paid more attention to my drink than the movie, though, so it didn't take long until I felt like I needed a cigarette. I had just quit smoking again for the third time, but the tension and nervousness of my voided existence pulled at me. I was falling apart, exposing my wound-up insides, and I needed to smoke.

In the new neighborhood, the only place I knew of that was open was a gas station eight blocks away at Holton and North. Holton was the Mason-Dixon line. The other side was shrouded in darkness. I would never cross it. I probably wouldn't even touch it if I hadn't been drinking. It wasn't a good idea to walk down Holton at midnight, but I did anyway. The rumors were racist and exaggerated. I was still scared.

I made it unscathed. There, in front of the gas station, on a bench free from ads, sat a man who asked me for money. I had no change, so I turned him down. "Do you smoke?"

"Of course."

"I'm going to buy cigarettes. You can have a couple." Compassionate compensation. After screaming through bulletproof glass I came back to the man, two cigarettes extended. I sat and smoked one with him because I wasn't ready to walk back yet.

"Hey man, what's your name?"

"Mike. Yours?"

"Kevin." He gave me a handshake normally reserved for the business deal of the century. "My wife kicked me out, man." He launched right into his problems.

"Why?"

"She's sleeping with my brother."

"That's messed up."

"Some other guy, I can understand, but my own brother? We grew up together."

"I don't know what to say to that."

"Have you ever had a broken heart?"

"At the time I thought so, but never anything like yours is now."

"How old are you?"

"Twenty."

"You've never had a broken heart. You're a kid."

"My girlfriend just moved to New York." Add that to my list of mental strife.

"That's rough, yeah. But guy, my own brother!" He shook his head and stared into space with a look in his eye that said he was waiting for God to give him an answer. God didn't even tell him to build an ark to stay afloat on the flood forming in his eyes. "It ain't right, a man crying in front of another man."

"Don't worry about it. I'm not much of a man."

"Don't say that. You're a man. Sitting down with a brother and having a conversation."

Neither of us knew what to say, so we kept sucking through filters until we were done. "You sure you can't spare a couple bucks so I can get a drink?"

"I need it for food. But you need a drink. I've got some

whiskey at home if you want."

"Really? You'd do that for me?"

"Sure."

We dove headfirst into the whiskey. "You got yourself a woman?"

"She moved to New York. We still keep in contact. I think I told you that."

"I got me a woman. Or maybe had one. She kicked me out. My own wife."

His eyes welled up again.

"She's sleeping with your brother. You mentioned it."

"Did I? Sorry, but it's on my mind."

"I understand."

"What do you understand? You're a kid."

"I can still sympathize."

"I'll tell you what. You want to learn? Get some real experience?"

"I'm open to anything."

"What you got to do is kick it with some older dudes. When you see these old guys chilling on the corner, playing checkers or whatever, go hang with them. Learn something. But man, and this is the important part, when it gets heavy, you got to walk away."

He reached for his cup and raised a toast to me. I couldn't neglect honoring myself, but knew I couldn't keep drinking, either. My liver was four hundred people crammed into a room with capacity for two hundred, so I lifted my cup to my sealed mouth and let the liquid caress my lips, begging for entrance.

At this point he began pulling the filters off the cigarettes he had invited himself to smoke inside. I wondered why my cigarettes weren't good enough for him in their natural state.

"How do you feel about this?"

"About what?"

"Sitting here in your own home with a brother."

"I don't see a problem with it."

"No, you've got to have reservations about this."

"I feel pretty good. Drunk, plenty of cigarettes and decent company."

"You ever hung out with a brother before?"

"Sure."

"The white man shouldn't feel comfortable with this. And I don't blame you either. My fellow brothers, they don't make it easy on us."

"What are you talking about?" Maybe it was my alcohol-ridden mind that couldn't think straight. Maybe he wasn't disparaging all black people.

"I got a job and I'm trying to help myself out, but my brothers, they steal and do drugs."

Racism was sitting right next to me. My mind was getting tossed around like a dead body in a hearse during a car chase. "You're stereotyping. That isn't fair."

"All I can do is talk about what I see, and I see my brothers being bad people."

"You can't judge everyone on the few. If I did that, then you'd be sleeping on the street tonight."

"I can sleep here? You're a good guy. If I were you, I wouldn't have me here. But I am here, so let's make the most of it." He lifted his cup in another toast. I allowed myself a small sip this time to help me cope with the beating my brain had just taken.

Like a toddler at his parents' funeral, I couldn't comprehend the gravity of my surroundings. Me: white and young, Kevin: black and middle-aged. Maybe I hadn't seen enough of the world. Maybe I was an optimist for thinking some form of unity could exist. Maybe I didn't understand how Milwaukee worked. Maybe segregation was a constant, necessary like oxygen or death.

"God, I need some pussy. You ever had a black bitch before?"

Racism and sexism in a polar vortex, pulling me in, creating a hole in the ozone of my consciousness. "Can't say that I have."

"Oh man, you're missing out."

"What am I missing?" I knew he'd tell me anyways.

He licked his lips before he continued, "I don't know if I can describe it." He reared himself up like a horse in heat and rubbed his palms together. "Those bitches go wild. Man, they love the cock. They live off that shit. Eat it up like corn on the cob. Know what I mean?"

"Not really, no."

"I knew I couldn't describe it. We should go get you a black bitch to suck your dick."

"I'm alright."

"We can walk two blocks and get you some. Get me some, too."

"What about your wife?"

He scrunched his face up, perplexed. "Ain't nothing wrong

with getting your dick sucked every once in a while."

"I'm good."

"Alright, a guy's night." Another toast. "But sometime, we're getting you some black pussy."

I shook my head.

"Let's go get us some weed."

My face went stone. "I don't want to do that." I had heard Onopa release its patrons into the night; it was after 2:00.

"I need this. You got me a little drunk, now let's get us a little high too."

I was perfectly drunk at that second. "How are you going to afford weed?"

"We don't need much. I saw that twenty. We'll just get a dime bag."

I had left my grocery money on the bed when I went to buy cigarettes in case I was mugged. When we got back, I snatched it up so Kevin wouldn't take it. "That's for food."

"I need some weed."

We said the same yes-and-no statements for the next five minutes until I changed the subject and said we should watch a movie.

"What you got?"

I took him to the basement and showed him. "What do you want to watch?"

"Something with a brother in it."

I had nothing. I was embarrassed and grabbed something, anything. I didn't care what, as long as it talked, so I wouldn't have to. Immediately after I put the disc in, he asked, "How about that weed, man?"

"Fine," I lied like concrete. I was done with this and drunk enough to think I was clever. I had a plan. Since he wouldn't give up his notion, I'd have to give up on him. I'd follow him to the front door, close it on him and turn the deadbolt, keeping my money, if not my dignity.

The plan was fine, but I wasn't. I had my hand on the door, feigning a step outside when I saw a man in a brown overcoat and green baseball cap sitting on my steps. My liver told my brain to stop and ponder this.

"Hey man, you got any weed?" Unlike me, Kevin took advantage of every opportunity.

"Yeah. I got that sprinkle, too. Let me in."

"We don't want none of that."

"I can't let you in," I started to close the door, but the new guy wedged himself into the jamb. I wasn't even close to being able to push him out. Kevin was on his heels.

Now I had two people on my bed looking to get high with my money. The new guy poured himself four shots and downed them one after another. I sat listlessly aside, watching events transpire in my own abode.

"Where's the weed?" asked Kevin the businessman.

"Where's the money?"

"He's got it."

They took notice of their host for the first time since reentering. "I'm not paying for this."

"Man, you said you would."

"How am I supposed to trust this guy? We don't even know if he has anything."

"I fucking got it, but you ain't going to see it til I see some money."

"No way." I stood with my arms crossed.

"Alright, man. Let's sit down and watch the movie," Kevin said.

We did. I sat on the ground, close to the doorway. It wasn't long before Kevin said, "How about you roll us up a joint of that stuff and we can sit back and really enjoy this?"

"How about he gives me some money?" He looked at me with eyes like a tiger on fire.

"You know that's not going to happen." My blood remained calm.

"Then we ain't going to enjoy this."

We made it about seven minutes before the new guy hit open, threw disc one on top of the TV like a teenager handling his backpack after school and popped in disc two.

"There's nothing but special features on that disc."

"Shut up, bitch." My blood was lukewarm.

We sat and looked at the special features menu while the guy tried to figure out how to use the remote. "This shit sucks." He gave up and started fondling the few possessions I had upstairs. His eyes gave away his sleight-of-hand intentions.

"Get off my shit!" My blood boiled over.

"Man, fuck you!" He went from prone to erect in the flash of a camera.

Kevin lumbered to his feet and formed a barrier between me and the guy. He pulled me into the kitchen. I kept my eyes on my roommate's bedroom. "You have to calm down," he said in a hushed tone.

"I don't have to do anything. This guy doesn't have shit.

Let's get him out of here." I matched Kevin's decibel level as best as my shrieking kettle would allow.

"Alright." He walked back to the bedroom and motioned for me to stay where I was.

I sat there long enough to cook ramen noodles before they came out, arm in arm like old war buddies.

"Okay man. We're going to go get weed, but we need money."

That was his solution? If I had to part with my money to get them out, then so be it. I needed them gone. "I'll see what I have for change." My laundry fund amounted to three dollars. I had a dollar left in my wallet from my earlier cigarette run.

"Four dollars ain't nothing. You said he had twenty." The guy threw a temper tantrum.

"I need that for food." I opened my refrigerator door. "See what I have? Soy sauce, almond milk and margarine." I didn't open the cupboards, which were fully stocked.

"I know you got some fucking money, white kid. What about that TV and DVD player? Your ass is packed with cash, bitch."

"I found them on the street." This wasn't true. They used to belong to my parents.

"You can find four more dollars. We can get a dime for eight. I know a guy. Then we can all calm down," said Kevin the mediator.

I went to my backpack in which there was a compartment with miscellaneous, essentially worthless currencies— Canadian quarters washing machines refused to take, Circus! Circus! poker chips my dad had given me and two two dollar bills. "Here."

The guy looked at the bills like they were species gone extinct. He was skeptical, but took the money and left.

I should have let it go there, but I couldn't. Instead I fumed like a combustion engine. The ignition turned and I exploded. "Motherfuckers!"

I was hellbent on reparations. I ran to the kitchen. I opened the lone drawer that had anything in it and pulled out the chef's knife I had bought at a church rummage sale a month before.

"What's up now, motherfuckers?"

The General commanding me yelled, "Secure the perimeter!" with enough force to collapse a lung. I obeyed and locked all doors and windows.

"Take the lookout!"

I opened the upstairs street-facing window and stuck my head out. I kept the knife inside. "Here nigger nigger nigger nigger. Here nigger nigger."

I throbbed at my post for a good ten minutes until my bloodlust got the best of me and I started pacing through the house, looking for a body to stab.

Eventually I realized I should have stabbed myself. "Calm down. What's wrong with you? They're gone for good. Remember to breathe."

I needed fresh air. I set the knife down by the door and stepped into the cool 3:30 air. I locked the door behind me for a meaningless condolence, like saying, "I understand," to a friend caught in a tragedy. I sat on the top step and lit a cigarette. Each exhale released my annihilation. I was almost done when the last thing I expected to happen happened; they came back. They already had my money and booze, what now?

"We got the weed, now let us in," Kevin said with the excitement of a child.

"No way."

The guy climbed past me and tried to push his way in again, but found that the lock was stronger than me. "Unlock this fucking door so we can smoke this shit."

"I'm not letting you in."

"What the fuck!" He turned into violence personified. His eyes went red and bulged. "Let me into this fucking house or I will wipe you out."

"No." My blood would remain calm, I promised myself. No more cheap racist shots I didn't really mean. That wasn't me, I told myself, but anger and booze.

"Come on. We went and got this, now you keep your end." Kevin was pleading.

"I gave you everything you wanted. Now get out of here."

"You told me I could sleep here tonight."

I didn't remember saying that. "No one's staying here." I threw my used-up filter and walked away.

Kevin followed. I didn't know where I was going besides away. "I'm going to sleep out in the cold. I need somewhere to sleep. I'm homeless, brother."

"That's too bad, because tonight I'm homeless, too. I don't know where I'm sleeping."

"Fuck you, man!" Kevin showed his first signs of violence. "This is some cold shit. You're just going to walk away?

Motherfuck you!" His words rolled out of his mouth like bullets off a bandolier.

I felt like a rabbit in the sights of an owl. I needed a bush to take cover under. The red and blue flashing lights of a squad car beckoned protection ahead on Locust Street. For the first time in my life, I was glad to see a cop had pulled someone over. "Leave me alone. I am heading for that cop. If you're still following me when I get there, you know you're fucked."

"You don't want to do that. I didn't do shit."

"Who do you think he's going to believe? The homeless black guy or the white kid?" I didn't turn around, but I knew he wouldn't follow.

Then came the matter of finding somewhere to sleep. I paged through the contacts in my phone, looking for compassion. Although he was a forty-five-minute walk away, past Brady Street, my future roommate Kyle was willing to temporarily house me. Yet another part-time living arrangement. He was awake when I got there. "What the hell happened?"

"Some shit, man. Serious shit. I'll tell you in the morning."

The sun woke me up at noon and I told him everything over whole wheat toast.

"I guess you learned not to trust people."

"Yeah, I guess."

Too shaken to go home, I made Kyle's my Sunday headquarters. When I came back into the house on Monday, I found a paranoid painter brandishing his brush like a club. "I live here," I said.

"I hear you were broken into." I went to my temporary room to gain my bearings. Everything but the bed was gone.

"Any idea what happened?"

"You don't know?"

"This is the first I'm hearing of it."

"Maybe the neighbors filed a report. We already fixed the window. I'm on my way out. Not quite done, but I'm exhausted. You should get some bars on those windows. Really, this neighborhood isn't too bad. It's on the way up, but it couldn't hurt."

Would I be keeping the world out or myself inside? "I'll think about it."

My doorbell rang Monday night while I was sitting in scared silence reading. My blood went ice cold. "Hey! Hey guy!" It was Kevin's voice accompanied by violent doorbell buzzes.

I dialed 911 with what little battery my phone had left. It rang seventeen times. I waited like an audience anticipating a hatchet in a slasher movie. I couldn't wait any longer. I called Kyle. "Can you call 911 for me? Kevin's back and I don't have battery left."

"Oh shit. Yeah."

Kevin got bored, decided I wasn't home or that it didn't matter how hard he rang, I wasn't coming to the door and left. I waited at the front window for the cops like a small dog awaits the arrival of its master. The flash of a spotlight came through the glass, and I knew master was home.

"We got a call about a potential break-in here?" There were two of them, one with a mustache and one clean-shaven. Both had the same buzzed haircut.

"I was broken into this weekend and I think the guy who did it was just here."

"How do you know?"

"I don't, but this guy knew I wasn't here when it happened."

"A friend of yours?"

"Not exactly. I met him Saturday night."

"A bar?"

"When I went to buy cigarettes."

"So you don't know him. He's gone now?"

Clearly, there was no one else there with us. "Yeah."

"What's he look like?" I knew he wanted me to racially profile Kevin. "Black guy?"

"Black. Kinda heavyset. He was wearing a green jacket, tan pants and a baseball cap. He should still be in the neighborhood. He headed down Fratney."

"So he's probably still around? How long ago was he here?"

"A few minutes."

"This is all about drugs, isn't it?" asked Shaved.

"What?"

"I want to know what we're getting into here. This doesn't make sense. You and a black guy you just met hanging out. Something doesn't add up. If you owe him a bunch of money for drugs and we're about to get shot at, I deserve to know."

"Nothing like that. The only time drugs came up was when he wanted to go buy some weed. I didn't want to and that's when I decided I wanted him out of here."

"How'd you get him out?"

"I gave him the money."

Shaved rolled his eyes to indicate I was clearly a hopeless human being.

The doorbell rang. Shaved pulled his gun instantly. I walked to the corner with my tail between my legs. My ears went deaf to my surroundings until Shaved came and talked to me. "Is that the guy?" He shined his flashlight directly into Kevin's face.

"Yes."

"Now why would you let a guy like that into your house? Look at him. He's probably twice your age. Don't you have any street smarts?"

"I guess not."

"No, I guess you don't. Stick to hanging out with buddies your own age. These guys know what they're doing. They get into your house, see what you have, and then come back later and take it all." I realized that nothing from the basement was taken. Kevin knew all that stuff was there and none of it was gone. "You know this guy's on probation for burglary?"

"I didn't know that." I started shaking. Everywhere. Uncontrollably.

Mustache finished with Kevin, left him outside and came to talk to me. "He says you guys went to the park and then he broke off and came back this way. He says he saw the other guy you were with breaking in and then waited for the cops and told them what happened."

"You let two of these assholes in together? College boy, do you realize two of them outnumbers one of you?"

"When I went to get the first one out, the second guy pushed his way in. I never wanted him here, but I couldn't call the cops because he would've heard and I'd be dead now."

"You know they were working together, right? Has your naive little brain realized that? Let me teach you a few life lessons here. Never give these guys money. They'll tell you it's for food and then go spend it on drugs. And never let them into your house."

Mustache saw me shaking and stepped in. "Do you want to speak with this guy?"

"At this point, I just want to be left alone."

"If anything else happens, call us."

Everyone thought they had taught me a lesson.

"Don't trust anyone."

"Don't show someone your money."

"Don't befriend strangers."

"You're an alcoholic."

"Beware black men."

But I didn't learn anything. Like the city itself, I would never truly change.

I Have A Mustache

I have a mustache. Until yesterday, I've never in my life had a mustache that stood alone on my face like the last soldier alive on a battlefield. Now, though, a mustache is necessary to my existence.

My mustache is red and kinky and wiry like pubes, but on my face; only the best of pubes are promoted up to my face: glorified pubes. It's a thick handlebar that starts on either side of the little palette below my nose and continues on down to my jaw. The hairs are long enough to reach past my first knuckle when I extend my middle finger and primitively measure.

I take my mustache seriously. When I look at myself in the mirror I think I look good for the first time in my life. No one under the age of forty looks good with a mustache. I am twenty-two years old. I have no intended irony in my rock-and-roll mustache.

Mustaches are designed to disguise. Before my mustache I had a beard; a great redwood lumberjack of a beard. Last week my boss asked me what I was hiding because she'd never seen my chin before. I wasn't hiding anything; I've just always been too unmotivated to shave. Now my chin is exposed and I am hiding.

My roommate Dave, his friend Jo Jo and I were walking to the liquor store just before Tuesday Movie Night festivities were to begin. Same liquor store I'd been to each of the three previous days. Jo Jo is a normally sized girl. Dave and I might reach three hundred pounds combined. Maybe. We are no bonecrushers.

A block from the liquor store, Justin called me to see if Movie Night was happening and where. "My house. You should come over," I told him. "It'd be great to see you."

And now I'm on the ground. I see my phone close and Justin's call is dropped.

Some thud happens on my leg.

I am being beaten, I realize but never actually think.

I've lost Dave and Jo Jo. I get up. I run across the street, noticing a cacophony of talking and yelling, but only being able to register, "Shit. Look at the bitch run."

I hit the sidewalk. I am thrown down. I sense boots and fists all over my body but feel nothing. This has already happened. This is happening.

Teenagers. A group of kids we passed before I was on the ground. They must be doing this to me.

My phone is still in my hand.

And now I'm standing again and my attackers are gone. I do not see them leave.

Dave ran up to me with his phone against his ear and said, "I'm sorry, are you alright?"

Pain was nonexistent. "Yeah. I can't see. My glasses are gone. Lead me."

"Can we go home please?" I asked when he started leading me toward the liquor store again. We should get the fuck out of here, I thought and crouched lower to the ground in an assassin's pose.

Dave was talking on the phone. He didn't hear me.

Jo Jo was waiting for us in the liquor store parking lot, also on the phone. So was a guy I recognized as the clerk once I got close enough to turn his blurry shape human. All three of them were having a round with 911, going through the same info one after another.

Jo Jo asked for my phone number and I told her. She told it to the phone.

Then there were three police cruisers in the parking lot and three men asked me if I needed an ambulance. "I don't think so." "I think I'll be okay." "No. I do not require an ambulance."

None of the cops had mustaches.

Two cars left and the one that stayed behind told us they were out looking for the suspects. I started to feel like I was watching *Cops*.

I called Justin and said, "Didn't mean to be rude there, but I just got jumped. You can still come over. We're at the liquor store filling out a police report. We'll be back soon."

Our cop took the report, pausing every few seconds to lecture us on how important police are and how the laws need to be tougher and nothing's going to happen to the kids and really this report's just a stat so they can justify raising the police budget so they can hire more good cops like him.

According to Dave and Jo Jo, there were about ten kids in total, four or five of which beat me. The rest—the girls—stayed out of it.

"That's one of the girls right there," Jo Jo said. "In the peach pants."

I couldn't see any peach pants.

"Stay here. I'll be right back," the officer said.

I pulled out a cigarette and asked with a smile, "Think this is going to hurt because my lip's split open?"

"Probably," Dave muttered like a secondary or tertiary thought coming to the surface.

It didn't hurt.

Justin biked up to us. I told him what happened; I'd heard Dave and Jo Jo tell it enough times that I was starting to feel like I had seen everything, that I knew everything, that I was a police report.

The cop came out of the store with the girl in handcuffs. He took her away from her friends and questioned her.

Her friends threatened us: "Oh, that's it. You guys are finished."

I smoked and wondered why the cop was bothering to put my life in danger for a statistic; I lived in that neighborhood and had a giant red beard, I would come across those kids again, they would recognize me and I didn't want them seeking revenge for snitching. I hadn't even called the cops. I just wanted to go home.

"You guys probably don't want to hang out here too long," Justin said.

"No shit, but he's still got my ID," I said.

"Does anyone at your place have a car? Can they come get you?" Justin asked. We told him yes and he biked to tell someone to come.

The cop came back without the girl and told us what he'd just done was illegal. He kept insisting that he knew one of the kids, some kid with red dreads and a black hoody, or no, maybe a red hoody, and weren't there a couple kids with red dreads, actually? And each time he tried to get me to identify one of the kids I told him I hadn't seen any of them; I would have told him the same thing even if I had seen.

I watched behind my back while he finished the report.

Just as the cop was clicking his pen cap back on, he said, "Wait. Did you say they broke your glasses? I can put that in here. If the insurance company gives you a hard time then you can tell them about this. I'll send someone to take a picture."

I had no idea how that string of sentences formed a coherent paragraph and I just wanted to get out of there with my life intact for the next few weeks. "That's okay. Have a good night."

"You sure?" He was stretching for something else to put in his report, something of monetary value, so he could show the stats to the mayor and hire new police officers, hopefully ones as life-threatening and law-breaking as him.

"I'm positive."

When I got home, everyone swarmed on me like I was a coffin with a dead celebrity inside. "Yes, yes, I'm fine," I assured them. "I think Dave's more shaken than me. He looks like he's seen a ghost," as he rightly should have after watching me get beat down. I was fine because I hadn't seen anything, hadn't even registered it really happened, except for a few dull throbs of occasional pain.

"Tina, could you shave me?" I asked her because she'd done all my haircuts since I first met her.

"Now?"

"Yeah. I don't want to look like me anymore."

Tina's boyfriend James went looking for my glasses and said all ten kids helped him find them. Maybe they thought they were lucky they hadn't been pursued harder by the police. Maybe they were sorry. Maybe they realized James is a big fucking dude and they couldn't fuck with him so they became respectful. James is a bonecrusher. "You kids need to chill out. No one needs that shit," he told them before he biked away.

And he came back with my five-year-old glasses, still intact and, now that they'd been changed and reshaped by violence, even better fitting than before.

A Human, A Robot

They're crying again. But no, they're almost always crying, so again isn't the right word: still. They're crying still. But they were just so quiet for thirty seconds, a minute—hard to say really. No longer. The important thing is that they're crying and it's my job to get them to stop. Or at least approach a more appropriate volume.

A roomful of preschoolers with snot and tears pouring out of them like dandruff off a head being massaged and what am I going to do to make them stop? Nothing. Kari, Jill and Tanya, on the other hand, are going to do everything they can. That's what I trained them for.

"Girls. It's getting kinda loud in here. Let's see what we can do to keep the noise level down, okay?" A question? No, a command.

And they all jump up and put blocks and trains in the little ones' hands and things calm down a bit. For a bit.

Although our website says the ratio is never higher than five children per daycare provider, there are twenty-one kids in the room right now—seven kids for each provider. The ratio is always disproportionate like this on the weekend when Mom and Dad are decompressing at Sak's or off trekking through some pseudo-nature experience. Suzanne can't convince more than a couple staff members to work weekends because they all think their days off should be Saturday and Sunday with the rest of the world and not in the middle of the week when they could actually go to the post office or grocery store without having to wait in line.

I don't count as a provider. I'm the Office Manager; I

handle the queries about our services all those potential clients ask, deal with the books, and am in charge of staff. Suzanne has more authority, power and responsibility than me —she's the owner—and she tries like glue to keep everything together around here. It's the weekend—her weekend, I should say—though, so I'm in charge. All decisions are made by me. Mostly that means telling the girls—men work here too, but only women seem to be available for the weekends— when it's okay for them to go to lunch.

Suzanne is so very L.A., but she's trying hard to get over it. Enough Botox to wipe out the whole city, nightly whitening strips, every fad diet that's ever existed, enhanced breasts, an obsession with her social status, but she's trying to change all this, to enrich her insides. That's why she opened this daycare center. The girls and I like to say she's a robot who's trying to die a human. She doesn't know we say this. She's making progress. I don't have to deal with those pressures; I'm from Connecticut and moved out here with my boyfriend (broken up now, but still in touch) a couple years ago for a change of scenery. I love L.A.

I've only worked here a year, but Suzanne, in all her benevolence, has already made me Office Manager; I've had the job for two months now. The promotion came with a thirty-five cent an hour raise. I know it doesn't seem like much, but after working here six months my pay skyrocketed a buck-fifty. And at two months, after I passed my probationary period, I got a dollar raise. So in one year my pay has gone up two eighty-five. And I get a week's vacation at half-pay. Not bad, huh?

"Cindy, can I go to lunch now?" Jill asks.

Everyone's relatively calm, so I say it's okay and tell the other two to watch over Jill's kids. I go back to looking up recipes for gumbo online. Can you believe what they put in there?

When I first started working here, I had to sign a sheet that said I'd read and agreed to the company Internet policy: "No unauthorized, non-work-related use of the Internet allowed," but Suzanne doesn't mind. She's seen me on Yahoo! Games before and hasn't said anything. As long as I get all my charges and stuff done, it's no big deal. And there aren't many charges to do on the weekend. The majority of the kids here today have prepaid accounts; most of the parents, with their spur-of-the-moment meetings and the need to be on-scene anytime, think it's easier to be able to drop their kid off whenever they want and not be hassled with having to bring out their credit card each time. Suzanne is more than willing to cater to their desires. I suppose I could help out the girls with lunches, but it's good for them to be on their own; when I first started, I had to handle fifteen kids all by myself. Things keep getting better and better around here. Most people don't even realize it.

Look at me, gushing about my job like it's as great as marriage or something. There are a few things I have problems with. Suzanne and I are talking about them though, and it's going great; she's really attentive and listens to my problems, even if she can't do anything to fix them. Like, for example, when someone becomes a client, she insists we keep their credit card number on file. I worry that someone might break in some night when no one's around or that one of the employees lied about his/her background info, changed their Social Security number and has committed identity theft before. And with that filing cabinet of 1,000-plus names and numbers, it wouldn't be hard to do again.

And she doesn't have a problem bending the truth, like with the website/actuality disconnect. Also, instead of telling Mom, "Tyler hit Stephanie in the face with a Tonka truck today," she says, "Tyler got a little excited today." Which means when Tyler's aggression gets out of hand (and it will, because Mom doesn't know about it and therefore can't do anything about it) and I have to tell Mom Tyler can no longer come, Mom takes her anger and aggression out on me. And we still keep Mom's card number on file.

"Cindy, I have to use the restroom, could you help Kari out?"

"Sure." I always help out when needed; it's what a good, caring manager is supposed to do. There have been Saturdays where someone called out sick and I had to spend all day on the floor and then stay late to do my charges.

"What would we do if Henry had a seizure while he's here?" Kari asks me. Henry doesn't come very often. In fact, this is his first time here in months. He has epilepsy; we give him meds each day he's here around lunchtime. None of us are EMTs and none of us would know what to do if it came up.

"I don't know. I'll ask Suzanne about it tomorrow."

I have to admit, although I love being Office Manager, sometimes I just want to hang out with the kids. This is why I work weekends, for those times Jill's on lunch and Tanya's in the bathroom and I get all the pleasure of the kids being excited to see me again without the hassle of crying and beating and inappropriate play.

"Holy jeepers!" I scream. "Tanya, get back out here!"

She doesn't come. Henry is convulsing. He's having a seizure. I freeze. Kari runs and grabs him. She takes him into the office.

Tanya comes out. "What's going on?"

"Henry had a seizure." I tell Tanya to stay with the kids.

Henry is still convulsing. Kari is curled up and crying. "I just said that ... "

"If you need to step outside, then do," I say to Kari.

"Are you sure?"

"Please. Go." She isn't helping anything anyways.

I hold Henry down, trying to get him to stop. His tongue flops out of his head. His eyes go blank. Three inches of drool hangs from his mouth.

Jill's in the office. "What should I do?"

"Call Suzanne."

She rushes to the phone like a firefighter after the bell sounds.

"Suzanne. Henry's having a seizure. What do we do?"

"No. He's stopped convulsing now it looks like."

"But he doesn't look good either."

"Okay. We'll call back in a bit."

"Call back? She isn't coming down here?" I scream and Henry twitches.

"She says to call Mom first."

"Okay. How about the hospital?"

"She didn't say to call."

I'm in the filing cabinet fast as a thief. Barrios, Henry. I know almost all the kids' last names.

I dial the number.

"Hello. Ms. Barrios?"

"Yes?" she says through a crackling connection.

"This is Cindy from Delightful Daycare. Henry's having a seizure."

"Yeah, he's about due. He gets them every six months or so."

Then what are the meds for? And why didn't anyone tell me this would happen? "What are we supposed to do? Should we take him to the hospital?"

"No. Just make sure he doesn't hit his head. He should come out of it in about an hour or so. If not, call me back. Ciao."

"She made it seem like no big deal. Apparently this is normal for him. Make sure he doesn't hit his head. I'm calling Suzanne."

"Suzanne, I could really use your help right now."

"I can't get away."

"Could you come down here please? I'm scared and I don't think I can handle this." Being direct is the only way to break through her programming.

"I'm sure you're fine. Mom said it was okay. Don't worry."

"He's seizing again."

"Just watch his head." Then away—distant—from the phone, "I'll be there in a minute." Back to me, "Goodbye Cindy dear."

"But ... " Dial tone.

"I have no idea what to do." I feel like I am shriveling up into myself.

"Tanya needs someone else out there. I'll go until Kari gets back. Just stay with him."

Henry seizes again.

I try to comfort him with my voice, cooing like naptime. He can't follow my sound; he can't see me.

His flopping slows. This seizure seems stopped so I go to the sink and get him some water. He drinks it down like there's a tube running down his throat; he doesn't really want the water but can't resist. He drinks the whole glass—at least what I don't spill—and I go to get him more. I splash cold, down-to-earthness on my face, and as I'm rubbing hydrogen and oxygen atoms into my pores, Henry thrashes again. He hits his head on the tile like dropping an egg.

The glass slips from my hand and shatters.

Jill comes back into the office. "Oh my God!" She has her hands underneath Henry's head. Or maybe her hands are there first and then she yells, I don't know.

Henry makes a hacking sound. His tongue hangs out of his mouth like fruit leather.

I see blood on the tile. "Is he bleeding?"

Jill says it's her blood, tells me to clean up the glass.

I bend down and pick up shards with my fingers. They splice into me like a chef's knife into a persimmon.

I feel blood spilling out of my fingers, from my cuticles, from my knuckles, from my palms.

I know Henry is going to die.

"I'm calling Mom again."

"Throw the glass away first."

I look at my hands. They have taken the glass into themselves; symbiosis.

"Ms. Barrios. This is Cindy from Delightful Daycare. Henry's having his fourth seizure now. He's not doing well."

"He's never had four before. Just give him an extra pill. That usually takes care of it."

"Could you please come pick him up?"

"Honey, I'm in the canyons. Even if I left now, I wouldn't be able to make it back before four, and he'll be fine in an hour. Just make sure he rests afterwards."

"I would really appreciate you being here."

"I can't. Goodbye. Good luck."

I grab a powdery white pill from the vial. His seizure is over. "Do we wait to give him this until he has another one?"

"Do you want to stick your fingers in his mouth then?"

"No. I can't pill him now, though. What if that was the end of it and Mom's right and he's done and we end up giving him an overdose?"

"That's got to be better than him having more seizures. He looks like he just fell down the Grand Canyon." Jill pushes the pill deep into his throat and plugs his nose to force him to swallow; he has lost all control of his own body.

"He's a wreck."

"Just one has to be exhausting; he's had four."

"How're Kari and Tanya?" I remember there are people, children, outside this office.

"Tanya's okay. Kari is pretty shaken, though. She keeps muttering to herself about clairvoyance. She's in no state to be watching those kids." The kids realize something serious is happening. They're all quiet and sitting on their hands.

"I still think we could use more help."

"Call Suzanne again."

I do. I get her voicemail. "I know she's screening me."

"Call someone else. We could use more people, regardless of who it is."

"It's the weekend; I'll never get anyone to answer the phone."

"Try. Leave messages saying it's an emergency."

The word emergency breaks me and I fall in the coalesced puddle of my blood and Jill's blood. I am crying. I feel like an exhaust pipe.

Henry seizes again. "Snap out of it and start calling people."

"Did he swallow the pill?"

"I checked. I didn't see anything left."

I gave him his pill earlier, I realize. I never checked to make sure he swallowed it. I keep this to myself and start futilely calling all twenty-six numbers on the employee phone list. No one answers.

Suzanne calls back. She recites the same motivational speech about how confident she is that I can handle the situation. She cannot see my red, swollen eyes, my mangled hands. She has not seen any one of Henry's eight seizures.

"We need to call the hospital," I tell her. She won't let me without Mom's authorization.

I know Henry is going to die or at least never be able to function the same way ever again.

The phone rings; it's Stephen. He's coming in. He says his little sister had a seizure before. At least someone who works here actually cares about the kids.

I look out into the playgroup and see more open space than before. "Where are all the kids?" I'm through the door, interrogating Tanya. Everything is going to pot.

"Parents are showing up and Kari's helping them out. Everything is fine. None of them realize what's going on."

"Where's Kari?"

"Outside. She's walking in with the parents when they come in."

I'm outside. "Are you okay?"

"I was just talking to my mom about this yesterday. My grandma used to be a famous psychic and medicine woman. My mom says this happens to her all the time, small premonitions that end up true. It's in my blood. It's my fault."

"It's no one's fault." I didn't check to see if he swallowed his pill. "We're doing all we can for him. You're doing great helping out the parents."

"Is Suzanne coming?"

"No."

"I quit. I'll stay and help today because I actually care about these kids, but I am never coming back here and dealing with her profits and not knowing a thing about what goes on at her own business. I mean, she owns this place! How can she not feel responsible, or at least liable, for what's going on in there?"

"I don't know. Just keep it up. The kids need you. I need you, okay? You're doing fine." Kari's absolutely right, I realize. This is unacceptable. This is Henry's life or death. This is my breaking point.

"It's not me I'm worried about."

"I have to get back in there. Come in later if you can."

Inside, Henry's seizing. "How many is that?"

"Eleven."

"Jesus. I can't deal with this."

The phone is in my hand. I up the ante and call Suzanne's cell.

No answer. How many times has she said in an emergency situation, call her cell and she'll always answer? "I'm losing it. He's still seizing. My staff can't take this anymore. Get in here."

We wait and watch Henry spasm. He looks like he has a thousand hearts, all pulsing arrhythmical at 200 beats per minute. We wait for Stephen, the closest thing to an expert we have, the closest thing to help. We wait for the hour Ms. Barrios spoke of to pass. We wait for Henry to get better. We wait for the end of each seizure. We wait for the next one to begin. We wait for Henry to die.

Things are running smoothly—smoothly like watching a plane majestically glide-crash into the ocean—when Stephen finally arrives. Kari and Tanya are on the floor. Jill is sitting with Henry, protecting his head and giving him water between seizures—he's up to twenty now—and I'm calling Suzanne every few minutes. She answers about every third call and says the same thing each time.

She is refusing to deal with the situation. She is forcing us to deal with the situation.

"Can you sit with Henry? Jill needs a break." I've relieved Tanya and Kari a couple times, but I can't sit with Henry; I can't be near him, I cannot touch him.

"Of course," Stephen says.

"Thanks for coming in." I'm crying again.

"How long since his last one?"

"The longest so far. Maybe ten minutes."

"Good. He must be coming out of it."

"Maybe." He looks catatonic, like he's in suspended animation in a beaker at some test-site in the middle of the desert. "I hope so."

"Anything different about the last ones?"

"No. But there've been a lot of them."

"It sounds like it's over to me."

"Can I leave you in here with him? I need to leave this room."

"Sure."

I sit at my desk.

I sit.

I sit.

I sit.

I sit.

I sit.

I sit.

Someone comes in. I don't recognize him. Kari's talking to him. She walks to the playgroup. He smiles at me. I sit. She comes back with Derek—he's here everyday. "Goodbye," he says. I sit.

I sit.

I sit.

I sit.

I sit.

I sit.

Stephen comes out and says, "It's been forty-five minutes. He hasn't had another. He must be done."

"Thank God," and I stand and hug Stephen like a hello-hug at a funeral.

"I'm going to go. Just let him rest and keep an eye on him."

"Thank you." I let go.

"Call me if you need anything else."

I can function again. I call Suzanne—"I knew you had it in you!" I wait for her to call me "Sport" or "Champ"—and Henry's mom.

"He seems to be coming out of it, but I'm not sure."

"Describe his symptoms."

"He looks desecrated—like he's a city where an atomic bomb was just dropped—his breathing is really sporadic, he's drooling enough to water the office ficus and he doesn't seem to be able to see or hear."

"Good. Perfect. That's exactly right."

"Are you coming now?"

"I'm leaving now. I'll be there right as you close."

She's going to be late, like always. "See you in a bit then, Ms. Barrios."

I go into the playgroup to let the kids comfort me, to allow their ignorance to clot my cuts, to hear them laugh and scream and kick and fight. Kari can handle the clients up front, Jill can sit with Henry, Tanya can keep the kids in check; I am going to play.

"Cindy, you need to get in here again."

I put down the See-N-Say and go into the office. The air is stale; I open a window.

"Something's not right."

"What's up?"

"I don't know, but he's not doing well. This isn't right."

I kneel next to Henry. There is red in his drool. "Why is he still drooling?"

Jill is silent.

"Is that blood?"

"I think so."

"Did he have another seizure?"

"He half-spasmed once. A bit ago, but I thought it was him kicking it out of his system."

"He's puking blood. Get me the phone."

I call Suzanne, who doesn't answer. "Emergency. Vomiting blood."

I call Henry's mom. "Oh. That's different."

"Can I call the hospital now?"

"Please."

"Thank you."

My fingers fumble between hitting end and 9—

"He's dead."

I look down. He's not breathing. I touch his chest to make sure. He looks like a dead deer, so peaceful and regal.

I put the phone down and wait for Suzanne to call me back; I know she will in about ten minutes. I am not calling Henry's mom to tell her. My line has been drawn and I will not tell Ms. Barrios this, not for all the wage increases or paid vacations or blind eyes to surfing the web in the world. It will take someone with the heart of a robot to break the news.

When I tell Suzanne Henry's dead, she breaks down and starts crying; finally, she loses a circuit and gains a left ventricle.

"She'll be there just after closing to pick him up, so we don't have to worry about a dead body being hauled out; would that ever look bad for business." She has a heart attack and her flesh needs to be replaced with more machinery.

"He's just going to lie here until then? Can't I call an undertaker or something?"

"This is what she wants."

"What do I do with him?"

"Cover him up. Light a candle."

"Are you coming?"

"There's really nothing I can do. I'll see you tomorrow. We can talk more then."

Handing over Henry's body, as lifeless as he is, is as lifeless as I feel, as lifeless as I want Suzanne to be. Mom seems to be okay, but she hasn't seen his body yet, either. His body, still covered in the blanket, feels hollow. I lift him into the cargo-bay of Ms. Barrios's SUV while she sits in the front seat, watching me in the rearview mirror.

Suzanne should not be alive. I've always given her the benefit of the doubt, thought she was trying to improve, to care, but Henry's death has shown me she will never become a true, good human being. Someone who distances themselves so far from death shouldn't get to experience the gift of life. She can replace her flesh with metal for all I care. She can come back to life as an actual robot, that's fine, that will make sense, but she is no longer a living, breathing, feeling, emoting human being. She never was.

Suzanne shows up for work an hour late. She strolls in wearing wraparound sunglasses, a long-sleeve lace shirt and jeans tight enough to be in a magazine ad. Her cellphone is up to her ear and she's smiling like the tabloids are watching her every move.

Suzanne spends three hundred dollars a week on catering and then lets most of it go moldy in the fridge at work. Today is split-pea soup with bacon croutons. She has me heat up her lunch each day and I add the botulinum I procured last night from Kari's grandma—Kari got me a discount on the condition I make sure Suzanne reads the fiery letter of resignation Kari wrote before she dies. Kari's grandma guaranteed that as long as Suzanne takes any amount at all, she will die.

She says she cannot squeeze me in until later, maybe towards the end of the day. It's a very busy day for her, I must understand.

"First, I want you to know how well I think you handled everything." A bowl with a few slurps of soup remaining sits on her desk. "I know you guys weren't equipped or prepared to deal with that. I want you to know I promise it'll never happen again. I can see how much it affected you."

Maybe it would've affected you, too, if you'd been within ten miles of the building.

"Walking in here today was like walking into a graveyard."

More than you realize.

"Now for the hard part. It was very much Henry's mom's decision to let him die. This is a right-to-life issue."

"What are you talking about?" Do I need to call poison control? Have I made a mistake?

"The last time she took him to the doctor she was told she needed to increase Henry's meds or he was going to die. She chose not to increase them."

"Why?"

"She said the pills took the life out of him."

Life? He's dead. "I can't believe her."

Suzanne tries to frown, but is unable to pull her lips fully down. She has always had trouble expressing emotion in her face, but this face is even less pronounced than usual. She looks tired. Her eyelids hang low. "She's not one of my favorite people now either."

"How is this right-to-life? Those issues are supposed to be about old people who're only barely classified as alive. Henry was full of life; there wasn't a happier kid out there."

"At least he was able to go happy, playing with his friends. Mom was really glad it happened here and not in the hospital." She drinks filtered water from a glass on her desk. A small trickle misses her mouth and slides down her chin. She seems not to notice.

"He'd be alive if he had gone to the hospital." My blood simmers with hate for Henry's mom for not letting me call an ambulance until she knew it was too late.

"Probably." My blood boils with hate for Suzanne for not letting me call an ambulance at all. For a second I was almost ready to forgive her, to put the blame squarely on Mom. Now I am clear.

"Isn't there an emergency disclaimer in the contract our clients sign that says we can take the kid to the hospital?"

"Yes."

"Then why wouldn't you let me call?"

"Mom seemed very cool about the situation. She seemed to know exactly what was going on."

"I was here! I knew! You had no idea because you refused to come."

"Relax. You're misdirecting your anger for her at me."

"You could have saved him. I could have saved him."

"I couldn't do anything."

There's nothing I can do to convince her, but still I scream, "Henry's dead! Kari quit! Henry's dead! What'll it take to get through to you?" Do you have a brain or a CPU?

"I couldn't do anything. Nothing could have changed this. It won't happen again." The ends of her words fall off her half-dead lips.

"No it won't." I get up with force, knocking over my chair, which hits a stack of papers. The toxin is in her system and she will die within the day.

I go to the filing cabinet. Barrios, Henry. 702 Apsley Way.

Mom's SUV is in the driveway. There's a lump of blanket—the same blanket I covered Henry with yesterday—in the backseat. I smash the tinted window with a shovel the gardener must've left out. It's Henry; pale, dead, decaying. He is no longer a deer, but roadkill; a raccoon or opossum.

I take the shovel into the house with me.

"What are you doing here?"

"Are you eating a fucking quiche?"

I slam Mom's face with the shovel and she falls to the marbled floor. I swing again, at her head. I take the point of the shovel to her throat and stand on it with all my weight. The shovel plunges through her throat like compost. I slowly drag her empty body onto the back step and leave her out to be eaten by the coyotes. I bury Henry in the yard and drop to my knees and pray for him.

I go home to mourn, to grieve, to try to die a human being.

North Oakland

Three or four beers into the night, our new roommate came home. Neither Quentin nor I had ever met her before we all agreed to move in together. But she had responded to our half-serious, half-joking Craigslist post we'd put up in desperation when our last roommate moved out on the 29th, drove a Beamer (had money for rent) and seemed at least halfway cool, so she became our third roommate.

"Hey Kate, how's it going?"

"Moving sucks."

Quentin and I toasted in sympathy.

"I need to get drunk."

"Pull up a chair and grab a beer."

"Is it okay if some friends come over?"

"Of course."

From the kitchen she said, "We'll need more beer. Can you guys go get it?"

"You want us to pay for your friends to get drunk?" Maybe this wasn't going to work out so well.

"No. No. I'll pay. I'm just not old enough."

"Wow."

"Yup."

I tried to remember being underage. I couldn't. Memory doesn't last more than five years.

To Murder Mart, lovingly nicknamed as such in honor of all the thugs that loitered out front. Mostly they minded their own business, at least nothing more than general empty threats, but this time one tried to start a conversation with us. More specifically, with Kate. "Hey baby, what's happening?"

Quentin and I kept walking. "Not much, what's up with you?" Kate was behind us now with eyes lit up like sales at Christmas time. She was in treacherous territory.

I had to act fast to get her out of there unharmed. "Hey Kate, come on and show us what you want." Safe for now.

On the way out, "You take care now, baby."

"See ya."

"Kate, where are you from?" I asked.

"Berkeley, born and raised."

"Hills?"

"Yeah."

I figured as much. "Have you spent much time in Oakland?"

"Not really."

"Let me tell you about this neighborhood. It's safe, really, it is, as long as you're smart about it. Like no conversations with people on the street. And no walking around by yourself. You're a girl. You probably won't get raped, but you will definitely be harassed."

"What is it about white girls with big asses for black men? I get it all the time."

"None of that matters. It's just that you're a girl and they're guys."

I saw her youth block my wisdom and gave up. Fuck it. Let her learn the hard way.

I went to answer the knock at the door. Ten faces that all looked about ten years old stared at me. "Whoa. Hey, how's it going?"

Coming in already, following their apparent leader, "What's up, is Kate here?"

"Umm ... yeah. She's inside."

After a round of introductions, I picked out my enemy for the night: Lucky, who looked exactly like my sixteen-year-old brother. Sample statements made by the small child:

As he was reading aloud the ingredients list of the soy crisps he'd bogarted, "Eating too much soy makes you grow tits."

"Hey fucker, toss that joint my way," and he proceeded to hoard the joint away from the rest of the room. I wasn't smoking because I lost interest in marijuana when I was his age.

"What tone was his skin, motherfucker?" Lucky asked the one black guy in the room after he told a story about some kid falling on his face trying to skateboard.

"What the fuck does that matter?" I finally exploded like a race riot.

"What? Was it like mine or like his?" he asked and pointed to the storyteller. The entire room groaned a sound of pity, remorse and fear. "Kid, it doesn't fucking matter." No one answered Lucky's question.

"Oh shit, I got you good, motherfucker."

Apparently he had insulted me; I was drunk enough to jump out of a window or light my hair on fire, so I don't really remember what I'd said to cause the impertinence or even what his abuse was based on, but the point is I challenged him with a "Shut the fuck up, bitch," which caused him to retaliate with threatening to fight me.

I knew the room was rooting for me over him, but I took the humane route and said, "Yeah, let's fight, and then afterwards we can whip our balls out and see whose are bigger. But you should probably go through puberty first to make it even."

He was ready to fight, on the balls of his feet, but his friends calmed him down. "Dude, you're a guest. Knock it off." They were mature compared to him. He was as near silent as he'd ever been in his entire life for the rest of the night.

The next day, Quentin couldn't find his drill.

"That fucking cocky little prick must've taken it."

"Kate warned me that he likes to steal shit, but I didn't think he'd take a drill."

"I fucking hate kids." So stupid he stole my friend's drill to punish me.

"And stranger-roommates."

"And work," and we left to go do something else we hated for the next eight hours.

Coming home from work, passing my local elementary school, my brakes started to squeal and my car was in the left lane before I realized a bicyclist had pulled out in front of me. I didn't feel the thud of a skull smashing beneath rubber and steel, but in the rearview, I saw a toppled black and pink mess.

Short of breath, I put on my hazards, double parked and got out, leaving the door open. "Are you okay?"

"I think so." She was a little girl lying next to a pink bike with shimmering tassels hanging limp like dead limbs from the handlebars. Fuck. "My knee's skinned, but that's it." We were both fighting off tears. I looked at the juxtaposition of bloody knee and black skin and my knees buckled. "It really hurts."

"Here. Let me give you a ride. You can't go anywhere on that," I pointed to the smoking rubble heap that was her bike. "And you're all banged up and it'll probably hurt to even try."

Scared, dazed and stupid—that's all she was, a dumb little kid who hadn't stopped at a stop sign—she got into my car. We left the bike in the road as a warning for the next motorist.

"Let's stop at the store and get you some first-aid supplies." I pulled into a twenty-four-hour drugstore. She stayed in the car while I got rubbing alcohol, Neosporin and Band-Aids.

While I dressed her wound with all the care of a mother bird, she stared out the window. Either I was truly gentle or she was tough because she never once made a peep of pain.

"Where do you live?"

"I don't know."

I was already on the road. "How can you not know?"

"I just don't."

Maybe she suddenly realized I was a stranger. She was a naïve little girl. "Well, where do you want me to take you?"

"Can I have some ice cream?"

How could I say no? I'd just about killed her, I could at least sugar her up and get her blood flowing again.

I hadn't gotten an ice cream cone since I was twelve, so I didn't have a clue as to where I might find an ice cream shop. I went to Safeway and got her an IT'S-IT. Again, she stayed in the car.

Headed north on Adeline, the same way she'd turned when I almost killed her, I said, "Where to now?"

"I don't know."

Her stupefied schtick was wearing on me, like a kid who won't eat his vegetables. "Look. I fixed you up. I got you ice cream. What more do you want from me?"

"I want to go home."

"Good. I want to take you there. Just tell me where to go."

"No." Her face was flecked with bits of cookie crumb. Sticky with vanilla ice cream smear and chocolate dip. She was a pitiful mess.

"Christ, kid," and I pulled over. "Do you want to just get out and walk from here?"

She didn't move her legs, just her arm to her mouth, so I took it as a no and started the car again.

I drove and she rode on in silence. "What were you doing

biking alone in the dark without lights?" I asked, and she didn't answer. "You know, that's not very safe." She didn't care that I was talking. "You need to learn to be aware of your surroundings. Hasn't anyone taught you that before?" Guess not, because silence equals no. I gave up being friendly.

I looked at her, sitting there torturing me for fun. Devoured that IT'S-IT. Probably does this all the time just to get the sweets her mom won't let her have at home, I thought. She was the one to bring up ice cream, not me.

God knows what she was thinking, but it was probably something like *Mmmm … I want more ice cream.*

"Either you tell me where to take you or I drop you off wherever I see fit." Goddamned kid didn't understand it's not free to drive around pointlessly. And now I was a good couple miles north of home. In Berkeley.

She licked the disgusting ice cream mess from her face without a word.

I turned around, headed south, then turned right into West Oakland. I pulled away from major streets so she wouldn't be able to find a busline, decided that wasn't enough, found an industrial alleyway and pulled in.

"Here. Get out." I wasn't far from where I worked.

She didn't move.

"Get out of the fucking car," I screamed, louder than even necessary to thwart off an attacker in a dark alley like the one we were in. When she didn't move, I reached for the Band-Aid on her knee and ripped it off. Still no peep of pain. "Jesus Christ! Can you even feel anything?"

She looked at me with big blank eyes like a fawn.

I reached across her and opened the door. "There. Get out."

"I want to go home."

"You had your chance, but you dicked me around and now this is where you live."

She just looked at me again.

I slapped her in the face, trying to force her out. Like she was glued to the seat, she barely swayed.

I got out and went around to her side and pulled at her arms; she was heavier than I expected—her weight like a dead body—but I managed to get her out. She fell over onto the concrete and didn't—wouldn't—move.

I started to sob and kicked her body like a dead dog or horse.

She started to whimper faintly like a baby who can't find her pacifier.

108

"So now we get a response. What else affects you?" and I sobbed heavy as a closed casket and kicked at her head. Her whimper became a cry of hunger, of innermost need. I kicked again.

"Stupid, stupid little kid, doesn't know anything about the world, about this city. This is the way it is." I got into my car and drove away. Left her there to die or live until she died in Oakland.

Janice, Her Roommate, And The Man They Do Not Know

Janice is being raped while her roommate watches. The man they do not know is of medium build, with short hair styled in a flattop. He says, "This is the best you'll ever have." His Dockers are unzipped, but not pulled down. Janice is tall and thin. Her hair is up for the night and she has blue eyes. She wears a violet robe. The roommate is short and naked and tied to a wooden chair with heavy rope. Her wrists and ankles are red. Janice and the roommate are both gagged with socks the man pulled from his jacket. The roommate's eyes are open; Janice's are closed; the man's are between these two states.

Janice shuts down. Everything she can, shut down. Neither her mind nor body are here for this pain and terror she cannot imagine, will not imagine. She is fine. She is limp, unresponsive, barely even a cell wall. Nothing is happening to her. Nothing is happening.

The roommate cannot turn away, cannot close her eyes. Immersed, the pain swells around her, inside her. Blood and oxygen flow through her. She exists entirely in this moment forever. There is nothing else in the world but the man raping Janice in front of her.

The man is forceful, quick. His muscles bulge with the contraction and expansion of power. This is what he is doing and he recognizes that. He grunts. He ejaculates and bows over, quivers, then zips his pants up, unlocks the front door and leaves.

None of these people will ever be the same again.

Everything Is Going To Be Just Okay

Sadie is Jimmy's female companionship. He uses her for all those tender, sensitive things men have women for. They've grown closer since Diana left. Sadie has been there for him, faithful as a wife at his side. She will not leave him. They are stable. They are forever.

Jimmy chucks the tennis ball dressed in saliva for his pit bull companion. She blasts off after it, dull pink tongue lagging out her mouth. She returns daintily, as though she hadn't just lost her faculties over something as simple as a ball. She is poised, like a woman should be. She drops the ball off in front of her master and waits obediently. "Good girl," Jimmy says as he scratches her chin. She is built and colored like a brick. He pump fakes to prove he is her master. He feels a twinge of guilt at humiliating and debasing her, but pushes it down quickly into the pit of his stomach. He throws the ball again.

He hardly ever brought Sadie to the park when he still had Diana, mostly when his boyfriend standing was in the doghouse or when he needed to take respite from Diana's onslaught of emotions. He picks the ball up off the arid dirt. His hand is filmy with slime. "How do you get this thing so wet?" He wipes his hand dry on his navy handkerchief, folded in his back pocket. "Let's go get you some water." He leads her to the faucet in the center of the park. Generally they stick to themselves on the fringes where few others tread. They are loners, only coming into the conundrum of people when Jimmy determines that Sadie is thirsty. Sadie laps down big, proud gulps of water from the lukewarm tap.

They trot back toward their corner, the corner where they and Diana spent the day on their "family excursion" a week before she left. Jimmy lobs the ball every few steps. He's sure to throw toward that blonde, still too far away to be sure, but she might be cute. She definitely has a set on her.

"She's so pretty. What's her name?" Jimmy had changed Sadie's collar from the generic leather one Diana slapped on to this pink one with spikes so people would know Sadie's a girl, but still tough, to devise an unspoken intimacy, an obvious femininity.

"Sadie." He tosses the ball. "Where's yours?"

She points to a German Shepherd kicking up dust clouds in the distance. "Seidon."

"Interesting name."

"My ex chose it." In part, Jimmy brings Sadie here to attract chicks. "I couldn't tell you what it means."

"My ex chose Sadie, too. I would've chosen something else, but well ... Here we are."

She pulls her sunglasses off and cleans them on the edge of her pink tank top. She reveals a sliver of tan, firm, bounce-a-quarter-off-it waistline as she does this. She's trying to get a better look at him. He flashes her his suavely mysterious smile. She realizes she missed a spot.

"What's your name?"

"Abbie."

"Jimmy. Sorry, my hand's covered in slobber." Jimmy is casual. Jimmy is nonthreatening.

"I understand."

"You and Seidon should join Sadie and me for lunch." He chucks Sadie's ball toward Seidon. He wants to encourage their dogs to interact. If the dogs get along then she will be forced to say yes.

"What the fuck!" Seidon is on top of Sadie, teeth in her neck like a blade. Jimmy is running. His chest is a combustion engine. His boots scream against the ground. His heart is somewhere else. His hands are wrapped around the dog's neck, wrenching scruff. The dog's teeth are in Jimmy's hands, back in Sadie. He rears back a steel-toed boot and crashes into the dog's chest. Again. Again. The dog lets up. Jimmy kicks again. Like kicking through an anthill or a bag of rotten melons.

"What are you doing? Stop!" She is coddling the dog, nursing his wounds. Sadie is still on the ground.

"Where were you? Fucking skank, control your dog."

112

"He's ball aggressive."

Jimmy's hands and wrists are covered in blood. His blood and Sadie's. Sadie's bleeding. "Your dog attacked my Sadie. Get out of here before I kick both your skulls in."

She stands there like she's waiting for an answer.

"Leave. Go." He steps towards them. They tuck tail and run.

Sadie is not standing up. Blood is beginning to pool on the parched grass. He grabs his handkerchief and does everything he can to stanch her wounds. He carries her to the car like a fallen soldier. "You're going to be okay, baby. Everything is going to be just fine." He drapes her across the backseat. He shouldn't, but he usually lets her sit up front with him. She is responding now, awake and cognizant. It almost seems like it's her back there.

She tries to stroll into the vet on her own paws, but Jimmy insists on carrying her. What a tragedy they must look like when they walk into the lobby. "Oh my God. What happened?" The receptionist is practically over the counter with concern.

"She got attacked by a German Shepherd." The blood is a lubricant. Jimmy almost drops Sadie out of his arms.

"I'll be right back."

Jimmy expected Sadie to be rushed back on a stretcher with a great sense of urgency; people clearing the way, screaming, tense, sweating. This is a waiting room.

The receptionist emerges with a blue bottle of something and a handful of tattered rags. "I'll take care of her. You go clean yourself up." Jimmy feels as though a cloud carries him. When he comes out, Sadie's neck is wrapped up.

She hands him a bottle. "Rinse out her wounds and change the bandages once a day. She should be fine."

"Isn't the doctor going to see her?"

"She's in surgery right now. Your dog will be fine."

"I want the doctor to see Sadie."

"That's not possible. We're really busy. Spring and all. The next available appointment is not until Tuesday."

Blood seeps through his bandages. "She can't wait that long."

"You really don't need to bring her in at all unless it gets infected, which shouldn't happen as long as you keep it clean and don't let her scratch at it. But call us right away if it gets any worse."

"How do you know she'll be fine?"

"I'm a semester away from being a vet." She rolls onto her tiptoes as she says this.

Jimmy knows what's best for Sadie, not this grad-school slut. His wrists are pulsating with pain, so he takes his elbow and jams it into her face. She goes down instantly. He sets his foot against her throat. "We will see the doctor today," he grinds through his teeth.

"That's just not possible. She's doing emergency surgery. Your problem, well, it's just not that serious. Nothing I can do about it." She's smiling like a waitress who plans on spitting in his chili. He presses down harder against her throat. She starts to gurgle out spittle like choking on a cock.

He doesn't make an appointment. He feels sick. His stomach feels like it's backed up, like it's been backed up for months. There is so much buildup. He will stop at the drugstore on his way home and pick up an entire first-aid kit and some antacid. He will clean Sadie's wounds. He will call immediately if there is any sign of infection. The receptionist smiles and waves at him as he leaves.

Jimmy peels off Sadie's bandages. Five days later and the gauze is still blood-stained. She should be healing by now. He rinses everything off with the solution the receptionist gave him and applies triple antibiotic ointment with a cotton swab. He puts down sterile gauze pads. He wraps around them with adhesive tape. He is careful to not make it too tight. This is the first thing he does when he wakes up each morning. This is the first thing he does when he gets home each evening. He then tends to his own wounds. His body is healing much faster than hers. He only wears the bandages as a sign of solidarity. Her pain is obvious. He is tender with her. It is only okay to be this way with her. Still, she whimpers when he dresses her wounds. He struggles against himself to keep from tearing up. He is unemotional. He is in control.

He will never again take her to the park. He cannot allow Sadie's well-being to be affected by others. If he ever sees that cunt and her dog again, it will be the last time anyone ever sees them.

They now take abbreviated walks. She'd hurt less off leash, but he can't bear her being more than a few feet away, can't leave her so vulnerable. He is her protector. Sadie is weak. She is nothing without him.

Jimmy is wary of the homeless woman wearing a hairnet, crouched and shitting in the distance, simply because she exists. He trusts no one. The woman starts barking as they approach. Jimmy sees her reach for Sadie with filthy fingers.

He lifts his leg and crushes down on her hand. He hears the satisfying snap and crack of bones breaking. She has learned her lesson. It's frivolous, but to prove his wrists are better, he takes his open paw and slaps her saggy weathered face. Instantly, it turns purple. He sees a rotted tooth fly out of her mouth. She is fully prone in her own filth.

He pulls Sadie close and quickens his pace. It isn't fair that Sadie has to suffer the consequences of the leash because some gutterslut tried to touch her. They rush home. Jimmy's not sure if he pulled Sadie away fast enough. That homeless whore may have touched her. He needs to clean her. Again. He peels off the bandages. Again. It seems like he's always peeling off the bandages. Again. Her neck is red and inflamed. He pours four antacid tablets into a glass and drinks.

Reluctantly, after the service he received last time, he calls the vet. "Just a minor infection, it sounds like," she says. "Our first availability isn't until Monday. She should be fine until then."

"You said she'd be fine before."

"How often are you changing her bandages?"

"Every time I clean her."

"And how often is that?"

"Whenever she needs it."

"Once a day. I told you once a day. Any more than that can encourage infection."

"I'll take the appointment." This is not his fault. He has done everything he could. He is sure of it. There is nothing else he can do. Sometimes things just go to shit around you and all you can do is watch.

Like a premonition, Jimmy knows her pain worsens each day. He's been following the vet's instructions exactly and Sadie isn't getting any better. Maybe if the vet had spent more than five minutes with her. That bitch did nothing to alleviate Sadie's pain. Jimmy is fully prepared to take matters into his own hands. He still has a bottle of painkillers from when he threw his back out. He never used them because he wasn't in any real pain. Not like what Sadie is in.

With hands desperate to make the hurting stop, he finds the amber bottle in his closet. He cuts the chalky white pill into two pieces and puts one of the halves on top of a bacon-style treat. Like a good little girl, she gobbles it down.

She is calm. She is sedate. She is at peace. She feels no pain. There is no pain for Jimmy in this moment. All is well in the world.

Nothing is better. Jimmy is in the waiting room of a new vet. Even though Sadie kept getting worse—puss, red, swollen, stretched, inflamed, engorged—they made him wait to come in until the antibiotics were gone. He is the only person in the waiting room. He smells the slickness of lemon solvent. This is more professional than going to the vet, like going to the doctor. Everything is clean and sterile, like no pain has ever been felt here.

"Sadie?" Jimmy stands and wipes his palms against the front of his jeans. "The doctor will see you now."

"What brings you here today?" This man is what Jimmy imagines when he hears the word vet: scraggly beard, big square glasses, trim hair parted on the left.

"They haven't fixed her." Jimmy turns Sadie's back to the doctor.

"How long has it been like this?"

"It's not getting any better."

"Has she been on antibiotics?"

Jimmy hands the doctor the bottle he dug out of the bathroom trash can this morning.

"And there's been no sign of improvement?"

"No one would believe me that she was worse."

"I'm going to call your old vet. I'll be right back."

When the doctor comes back in Jimmy says, "She's in pain, Doc."

"I'm going to look her over a bit more. Do some tests."

"Please fix this."

"Serious," Jimmy hears.

"Pain."

"It spread," brushes against his ear.

"Strangely unresponsive."

"Maybe last chance."

"Surgery." No one's lips are moving.

"Expensive." He hears the number five thousand.

"Chance of it being effective and then there's potential for infections for the rest of her life."

"For the rest of her life?"

"It's possible."

"And painful?"

"If it happens."

"Five thousand?"

"Around that."

His heart can only extend so far. He can only do so much. "I don't know." He won't say it.

"It is an option. We never suggest it, but we will provide it for you. Would you like to talk to someone about it?" The doctor sounds relieved to be rid of Jimmy.

"I need to consider all my options." He is making the wrong decision. He is making a thousand wrong decisions.

After the doctor leaves, Jimmy slips Sadie one of the painkillers he brought along.

"This is your choice." This woman is what Jimmy imagines when he hears the word psychologist: dirty blond curls, expansive brown eyes, tired lines streaking across her face. "What we would do is inject her with an overdose of anesthesia. She won't feel a thing. You can be with her for it if you'd like. It is a humane option. She might let out a cry but that's just the shock of the medicine flowing through her. You have several options for afterwards. One: you can take her home for a private burial. Two: a communal cremation. Everyone is cremated together and then you'll get back some of those cremains. Three: you can do a private cremation where she'll be the only one. Obviously this is the most expensive option."

Jimmy needs to have her forever. He nods. He cannot lose her, too.

"The private cremation?"

"Can I have a minute to think about all this? Could I have a cigarette before you do this?"

Jimmy walks through halls made of water. The sun is out. He can't tell if it's hot. He lights a cigarette and sits on his bumper. Does he have any other choice? It is the humane option.

An elderly couple holding shopping bags walks up to the car next to him. The lady opening the driver's door coughs to tell Jimmy he shouldn't be smoking in her vicinity. Jimmy burns his cigarette into the back of her neck. He erupts her hair in a burst of white flame. She is easy to push down, like a dream. Her flaming skull falls into the door frame. He slams the sleek metal shut. Again. Her husband watches. Jimmy takes a drag of his cigarette. "You shouldn't be parked here. You weren't at the vet. People need these spots. Maybe there's an emergency." The husband still stares. "Get out of here."

They get into their car and drive away. Jimmy goes back inside. "Okay," he says. "I'm ready."

Jimmy is driving. Jimmy is not sure if he's driving. He recognizes this as motion. Maybe the world is moving. He is staying in place. The traffic light changes. His foot stays. The world is flat, dull. Nothing is moving except those guys in white cargo shorts and baseball caps. They are singing. They are drunk. They are on Jimmy's car, pounding rhythmically. Their mouths spit against his windshield. Jimmy's door is open. He is outside, toe to toe with one. Pregnant with violence, he reaches back and swings. A dull thud, not at all what he was expecting. The frat boy hardly even stumbles back. They are on Jimmy. There are fists in every nook and cranny of his body. He recognizes the metal of his hood as hot. The sear of flesh and of pain. Real, very real, too real. "Fucking bitch," they say. "Little fucking pussy." They walk off, arms interlocked like champions, singing at top volume.

Jimmy peels himself off his hood. There is blood in his mouth. There is blood in his nose. He tastes the copper running out of him. He can feel himself pouring out. He gets back in his car and drives away. Nothing can ruin his pain.

By now, the bags under his eyes look forced. His contusions only swell and grow darker. He has not gone to work. He has not slept. The headaches don't go away. Nor do the gutaches and diarrhea. The dehydration is permanent. He sits by himself in his green plaid armchair. He smokes. His throat burns, but no more than any other part of his body.

He knows he has to try to move on, to act like he's okay. He's not. It kills him to admit this. Everything around him is ending. Diana left him because his emotions were walled off, she said. He never expressed himself, never told her he cared, that he loved her. He had a better relationship with Sadie than with her, she said. He misses Sadie.

He calls Diana and gets her machine. "It's Jimmy," he says. He cannot hold back the tears. "I had to put Sadie down. She got a really bad infection. It spread all over and they were going to have to do surgery. It might not have worked. She was going to be in a lot of pain for the rest of her life. I had to. She didn't deserve that. I thought you should know."

The phone rings as soon as he hangs up. "Jimmy? I'm so sorry. Is there anything I can do?"

He knows it's unfair to ask. All he wants in the world is for her to hold him and tell him everything is going to be fine. She has to.

"I can't do that."

"That's all I need. That's it. No more."

"I don't need that sort of complication in my life."

"I didn't need this in mine, either."

They hug at the door. Her smell comes back to him. Lavender. It smells so calm. "Thanks. This means a lot to me."

"You did everything you could."

"I know."

"You made the right choice."

"I know."

"That doesn't make it any easier, though."

He is crying in plain sight. He knows she can see him crying.

"Here. Come here," she says as she wraps her arms around him. "Everything is going to be just okay."

Words are meaningless. His tears staining her silk blouse, that's what matters. His arms wrapped around her waist, that's what matters. Her hand rubbing up and down his back, that's what matters.

"This isn't fair. She was so good."

"I know."

"She didn't deserve this."

"I know."

"We didn't deserve this."

They are in his bed, naked, sweating and relieved. As though their sweat released all the toxic shit from their systems. Their arms are wrapped around each other. Her head is tucked into his neck. "This might be good for you, for us," she says. "You've tapped into emotions you never had before." He faces the bedside table. He sees the picture of himself, Diana and Sadie from their trip to the park. All he wants is to hold her. He can't. All he wants is to cry. He can't.

Scenic Utah

To the best of my knowledge, I've never before been in Utah, but this all seems so familiar, like home. The open space like nothing else. Salt mountain mines. Long, slender washes of saltwater, ice blue over the soft, flat sand. Enticingly full of death. Horizons you could swim through. Distance further than the eye can see. The expanse of the crisp Salt Lake, like the Great Lakes I grew up with. The city itself felt like seeing an old relative, as though Salt Lake City were all those people swarming around the pool at the family reunion my grandmother once took me to. I didn't even stop, my car still moving like flipping through a photo album.

And then it strikes me. A memory. Those waves that bend the road's shine into metal are heat rising up from the asphalt. The sun beating down, attracted to the color, but also to everything this high up. My grandfather, my mother's father, taught me this while I sat, short-legged and smiling bright in pale skin, in the passenger seat of his semi. I remember my flesh—nearly matching pigments with the water —brushing up against the Salt Lake. My grandpa, with mustache and off-gray cap there at my side, watching me, sometimes me watching him and learning things of or out of this world. Everything is so real, like flesh. The body remembers what the brain cannot. Few genetics were passed down to me from him, but this memory is there, his memory is there; I've simply inserted myself into his past. Like how my grandmother and I drink coffee so long as we're awake, here is this part of someone else in me.

I grab my cell phone. My mother is speed dial two. With

road this open, I don't fear an accident. Sometimes she is greatly excited to hear from me, as though my voice could only bear good news. Other times, like now, she recognizes I can only represent the hideous truth. I tell her of my body memory.

She doesn't respond for the length of a salt flat. When she speaks again her breath is shallow and quick, like a widened creek. "I have to tell you something," she burbles. "I probably shouldn't. You shouldn't know, but I have to tell you." She pauses like she wants me to ask for her statement, but already I know I don't want to hear it.

"You are your grandfather's son. He raped me. Eventually I got pregnant and then there was you. I wanted to put you up for adoption, knowing you'd always remind me of that part of him. He didn't want that. 'No child of mine's gonna be raised by strangers,' he said. When he found out I was talking to the adoption agency, he went berserk. Finally, once, after making his nasties in me, he said, 'I'll stop this if you raise that child.' True to his word, he never did it again."

How she's lost contact with her father, has always seemed predisposed against him. How he seems to favor me over my brother and cousins. He always had extra candy for me when he'd come to visit.

"For a month I went around sleeping with every boy in town, desperate to convince one he'd knocked me up. Gosh, that sounds awful. I needed help. I was seventeen and not straight in the head. I needed protection from your grandfather too." I pull over onto the semi-wide shoulder.

"Your dad did good by you. I always figured he knew once he sobered up, but he stayed till you were gone. And still, he's good to me and my family too. Pays his alimony and calls my mom on Mother's Day. He doesn't resent me or you or anyone, and that's an unhuman pursuit." I push the button to methodically roll down the windows. The outside air is hot, stifling, unreal, like breathing liquid metal.

"Usually I don't believe in anything that can't be put in front of my eyes, but I believe this, you. Have to. Utah was always his favorite drive. Said you wouldn't believe all the scenery they got there. Sounds like you really like it, too."

I'm outside, sun beating down orange on my skin, walking through the crunch of the salt field. One giant hop to the side then I fall straight back, thousands of jagged little crystals stabbing into my body.

I learned this easily growing up, though I was never

very good. Arms and legs in motion. Now, this is the tricky part: stand up slow and delicate, get out before everything is destroyed, leap and turn. Salt angel.

Mike Bahl was born and raised in Southwest Wisconsin. He now lives in Oakland, California. This is his first collection of stories. He contributes to the fiction review blog The Heart Of Literature at http://heartoflit.wordpress.com. Sometimes he tweets at @mikebahl. He tries to be a good person, but is probably not.

Made in the USA
Middletown, DE
02 November 2022

14007537R00076